D0539160

Mr Barrett's Secret
and Other Stories

Fiction

Lucky Jim
I Like It Here
That Uncertain Feeling
Take a Girl Like You
One Fat Englishman
The Anti-Death League
The Green Man
I Want It Now
Girl, 20
The Riverside Villas Murder
Ending Up
The Crime of the Century
The Alteration
Jake's Thing
Collected Short Stories
Russian Hide-and-Seek
The Golden Age of Science
    Fiction (*editor*)
Stanley and the Women
The Old Devils
Difficulties with Girls
The Folks That Live on the
    Hill
The Russian Girl

Omnibus

A Kingsley Amis Omnibus
(*Jake's Thing, Stanley and the
    Women, The Old Devils*)

Verse

A Case of Samples
A Look Round the Estate
Collected Poems 1944–79
The New Oxford Book of
    Light Verse (*editor*)
The Faber Popular Reciter
    (*editor*)
The Amis Anthology (*editor*)
The Amis Story Anthology (*editor*)

Non-fiction

New Maps of Hell: A Survey
    of Science Fiction
The James Bond Dossier
What Became of Jane Austen?
    and other questions
On Drink
Rudyard Kipling and His
    World
Harold's Years (*editor*)
Every Day Drinking
How's Your Glass?
The Amis Collection:
    Selected Non-Fiction
    1954–1990
Memoirs

With Robert Conquest

Spectrum I, II, III, IV, V
    (*editor*)
The Egyptologists

With James Cochrane

The Great British Songbook
    (*compiled*)

MR BARRETT'S SECRET
AND OTHER STORIES

Kingsley Amis

HUTCHINSON
London

To Judy and Dick

Copyright © Kingsley Amis 1993

The right of Kingsley Amis to be identified
as Author of this work has been asserted by
Kingsley Amis in accordance with the Copyright,
Designs and Patents Act, 1988

All rights reserved

This edition first published in 1993 by
Hutchinson

1 3 5 7 9 8 6 4 2

Random House (UK) Ltd
20 Vauxhall Bridge Road, London SW1V 2SA

Random House Australia (Pty) Ltd
20 Alfred Street, Milsons Point, Sydney, NSW 2061, Australia

Random House New Zealand Ltd
18 Poland Road, Glenfield, Auckland 10, New Zealand

Random House South Africa (Pty) Ltd
PO Box 337, Bergvlei, 2012, South Africa

A CiP catalogue record for this book
is available from the British Library

ISBN: 0 09 177890 5

Photoset by Deltatype Ltd, Ellesmere Port, Cheshire
Printed and bound in Great Britain by
Mackays of Chatham PLC, Chatham, Kent

Contents

Mr Barrett's Secret

I

It must have been in the January or February of the year 1845 that I first became aware of the connection of Elizabeth, my first child and eldest daughter, with the man Robert Browning. Had I had the least intimation of what was to follow, I should have forbidden its continuance in any form, and have prosecuted my interdiction with unswerving tenacity. Nevertheless, full knowledge of the future that awaited Elizabeth and myself would surely have led me to bless that divine provision whereby it is not given to us to see as far as the next tick of the clock.

A letter, addressed to Elizabeth in a strange hand, arrived by the early morning delivery at my house at 50 Wimpole Street, a circumstance in itself very far from unusual. More especially since the publication by Moxon of her *Poems* in two volumes the preceding August, my dearest Ba (to use her family pet-name) had grown used to receiving correspondence from persons unacquainted with her. Many came from America and other distant parts of the world; the letter in question had been posted in London.

In characterising just now the style of the writing on the envelope, I used the word 'strange' advisedly. It was not only unfamiliar to me; it was peculiar, extraordinary, odd. And yet in its very singularity there was a principle I seemed to recognise from some distant part of my life, from long ago. Possibly, too, I was aware of an indefinable threat or menace lurking in it, remote but real; more likely, however, I am allowing later events to sophisticate those first memories.

Whatever I might have thought, then or afterwards, there was no doubt that Elizabeth was delighted with her letter. I had scarcely finished breakfast before I was urgently summoned to her room on the third floor of the house.

'Dearest papa!' she cried, rising from her sofa-bed to embrace me in lively fashion. 'You will never guess what a marvellous gift I have had in the post this morning!'

'You are bidden to take tea with our young Queen,' I suggested, smiling.

'It's a trifle soon for such a thing, though doubtless that and much else will come in time. No, I am recipient of a poem by Mr Robert Browning, a most beautiful and wondrous poem in which he exalts me to the status of a queen, but a queen of poetry and of the making of poetry. Oh, it's such a poem, darling papa, so full of the loveliest affirmations of devotion, so eloquent, so rich in the spontaneous vitality you know I prize above everything.'

'And this comes unprompted? As a spontaneous tribute?' I asked.

'Not quite, it's true. You may remember that in my poem "Lady Geraldine's Courtship" I referred to Mr Browning along with Mr Wordsworth and Mr Tennyson as a man whose writings place him next to the Gods.'

'So you did. And now he sends you a whole poem by way of return.'

'Well, there of course,' said Ba merrily, 'uncultured fathers and others of a sad literal disposition of mind will insist that the thing's only a letter, you know, nothing but a rather long and flowery letter, dash it all, the work of some modish popinjay with a fancy for extravagant compliment,' and the dear girl's voice and demeanour became for the moment a fanciful but truly comical travesty of my own. 'But this is a letter with the beauty and tenderness of a poem, a true poem. Enough! – you shall see and judge for yourself,' and she made to hand me the closely written pages, but snatched them quickly back and read from them in a high thrilling voice, ' "I love your verses with all my heart, dear Miss Barrett," oh, and, "Into me it has gone, and part of me it has become, this great living poetry of yours," and a little farther on . . .'

'I shall never see to judge for myself,' I laughingly protested, 'if you persevere in your recitation,' but I believe she was too much engrossed in those pages to hear me.

'Yes, he speaks here of, h'm, h'm, "the fresh strange music, the affluent language, the exquisite pathos and true new brave thought," and again, "I do, as I say, love these books with all my heart – and I . . .", but there I think he goes too far.'

A blush mantled her pale cheek. What had Browning written that she had not cared to let me hear? I know not, for I never saw that letter at last. But some of the phrases in it that I had been permitted to hear, the references to fresh strange music and to affluent language (affluent! a curious epithet, many would say, in this connection), remain lodged in my mind to this day. So did the general kind of expression employed therein. Once again, I felt I had received a warning or a premonition; once again, however, I may in saying so be looking ahead to what then lay in the future.

Certainly, at the time my strongest feelings were pleasure in my dear Ba's pleasure, heightened by satisfaction that her gifts of versing had been recognised by one I knew to be a poet of sorts, and by a reasonable hope that there might lie distraction from the melancholy and low spirits that had afflicted her increasingly as she grew past her first youth – at this time she was approaching her thirty-ninth birthday. My main concern, however, was as always for her health. This had never been truly sound since, at the age of fifteen, she had fallen victim to a mysterious incapacitating ailment that also afflicted her two younger sisters. As it proved, they were able soon to cast it off, but Elizabeth perhaps never wholly recovered, and within three months she had developed measles. Thereafter she spent much time confined to her room, even her bed, and I have always thought that the resulting seclusion and immobility were what first led her to the writing of verses – a healthier remedy than the opium which she came to consume, sometimes, I fear, in distressingly large doses.

Elizabeth's first letter to Browning further cheered me. I had been concerned lest, with all the refreshment of pleasure and interest in life the man's words might have brought her, she had perhaps become over-excited thereby, brought to an unhealthy access of sentiment. The dry terms of her answer, composed without any assistance but confided to me, were greatly reassuring. She spoke of her high respect for Browning's own ventures into poetic composition, saluted him as a fellow-craftsmen, told him that he would remain in her everlasting debt if he would draw her attention to faults in her manner of composition – nothing of the dreamy palpitating stuff in which he had evidently indulged himself. The correspondence continued. I had pressing concerns of my own at that time, in the City, relative to my affairs in the West Indies, and to be candid I was not sorry that my dearest Ba seemed to have found someone who might unwittingly share the burden of emotional obligation to her that I had inescapably (if gladly) acquired.

So matters stood for a couple of months and I was more than content. Elizabeth had acquired a companion who might prove more durable than her poor much-loved brother, known to her as Bro, lost sailing off the Devon coast at the age of thirty-three, and one who was nearer at hand than the excellent Hugh Stuart Boyd and John Kenyon, the latter known to me since our days at Cambridge and Elizabeth's benefactor and distant kinsman. Her letters to and from Browning, of which I was told nothing of substance, grew more frequent, but I saw no harm in that.

Then, in May of the same year, 1845, the two were to meet; he was to visit her at two o'clock in the afternoon of the 20th. I raised no objection; at that time I had none to raise; at two o'clock that day I was engaged in the City of London. I had left my Ba in her room as usual reclining on her sofa, surrounded by her simple furniture, most notably her beloved books on shelves built by her brothers, and with her spaniel, the well-behaved Flush, close beside her. As her father I could say to myself that, for all her large brown eyes and splendid thick dark hair, she was not what the world would have called beautiful. The black silk she wore at this season accentuated the pallor of her ivory complexion. She looked small and defenceless (she stood only an inch over five foot), eagerly desiring and yet deeply dreading the advent of the scoundrel* who had so artfully insinuated himself into the very springs of her being.

---

*Note: I am now satisfied that the abusive term *scoundrel* is unjust, together with the following clause, and that they represent nothing more than a transient, though once deeply felt, emotion of mine. – E. B. M-B.

Before I departed, I counselled Elizabeth to remember that this young man, six years her junior, must be as apprehensive as she of the coming encounter, and that, whatever might betide, he ardently desired her welfare, and doubtless more. What else could I have said or done?

'I see that Mr Browning's visit was a success,' I remarked some hours later as I took tea with Elizabeth in her room.

'Oh yes, it was most pleasant and valuable,' she replied from her seat on the sofa. (I occupied the armchair by prescriptive right.)

'How did he impress you?'

'He was most affable, and from the beginning there were no constraints. We had lively talk for something above an hour.'

'Upon what topics?' I asked.

'Oh, a great many, from poetry to politics.'

'Very likely. I was hoping you might particularise a little.'

'Oh . . . ah . . . he renewed his affirmations of regard for some of the things I've written, especially . . . especially "A Dream of Exile" and "The Rime of the Duchess May" and others. Truly, he was most . . . I could not have wished for a more . . .'

'No lady,' said I with a smile, my hands on my knees, 'is on oath when her father questions her on her conversations with an eligible young gentleman; indeed, she need say nothing at all. But, my dearest Ba, you and I have always been closely attached; pray do a little to indulge the curiosity of an old man and a loving parent. No doubt Mr Browning did converse with you of this and that; but what did you make of him, in what frame of mind do you look forward to his next visit, if there is to be one, did you like him?' And Flush, at her side as always, raised his dark liquid eyes to hers as if to say that

6

he, too, would have welcomed some information upon this head.

She looked at me for a few moments in silence, and it was not hard to imagine something of the battle of emotions that raged within her. Then she rose to her feet and held out her arms to me, and we embraced; I remember thinking how thin her small frame was, like a sheaf of ropes. Urging Flush to make room, she drew me down to sit close to her on the sofa and took my hand in hers.

'Dearest papa,' she burst out in her high voice, almost as thin in its way as her figure, 'Mr Browning is such an impressive, inspiring man, he has quite bowled me over with his ardour and strength. I swear that within a minute of his arrival I was in continuous suspense to see what he should say next – I learnt what it meant to be hanging on someone's lips. He carried within him so passionate a flame that I felt almost scorched by it,' etc., etc.

'I gather from this that you do wish to see him again,' I interjected when I thought it timely.

'I am quite set on it,' and she went on without pausing for breath, 'and this, all this, from a great poet, many say the greatest of our age!'

Soon I had seen and heard enough for the time being. In a light tone I counselled the dear creature not to allow her thoughts to proceed too fast, to beware of placing an extravagant hope upon the sequel to a single brief meeting, and to consider that Mr Browning must have many other concerns in his life than an occasional visit to a fellow-rhymer, however highly regarded. When she seemed calmer I left her. I had some thinking of my own to do, and a hope hardly less extravagant than any of hers to consider.

For despite the very great depth and strength of my

fatherly love, and the warm affection in which I had always held her, there was no gainsaying but that Ba's feelings for me, however welcome and however takingly expressed, were inappropriate in their degree. To put the matter in less abstract terms, she was nearly forty; while delicate of constitution she had the inner power of endurance shown by many other members of her sex;* as just demonstrated she was by no means indifferent to male charm; the isolation in which she lived was fully explicable but unnatural. To put it coarsely and more shortly still, she needed a man.

Perhaps Robert Browning was destined to be that man. For the time being I tried to look no further into the future. Mr Browning's letters continued to arrive at 50 Wimpole Street at an accelerating rate, and so did he in person for strictly delimited weekly visits. Dear Ba looked forward to each with what I may perhaps term a steady crescendo of expectation. She seemed happy. Her health was visibly better than it had been for years. All the same, I knew that there was more than a salubrious concern in her expressed desire, expressed indeed in previous years but never so pressingly as now, to winter out of England, in Malta, Pisa, Madeira. I would listen to any suggestion. Not having it in my nature to be either inquisitive or effusive, I was content meanwhile to allow matters to take their course. Nevertheless I knew my daughter was aware that, at least in principle, I was not unfavourably disposed to her association with the man who admired her so extravagantly, though I did wonder a little at not being invited to meet him.

---

*Not by any means all of them, alas. My dearest Mary, Elizabeth's mother, had died seventeen years before this at the age of forty-seven. – E.B.M-B.

II

That September, I was dining at the Reform Club, to which I had been elected a few years previously, when I was delighted to recognise my old friend John Kenyon at a nearby table. We arranged to take a glass of claret afterwards in the gallery on the first floor. His large, stout figure was soon seated opposite me. A half-bottle decanter of the wine arrived and we filled and raised our glasses.

After we had exchanged one or two trifles of family news, he asked after Elizabeth, with whom as I have said he was remotely connected, his great-grandmother having been the sister of Elizabeth's great-grandfather. Kenyon had been most kind and helpful to her in the past, encouraging her in her poetical work, visiting her frequently and introducing her to Wordsworth, an old man then though not yet Poet Laureate, and to Miss Mary Russell Mitford, authoress of that famous book, *Our Village.*

'Elizabeth is well,' I told Kenyon in answer to his inquiry. 'Her cough is always diminished in the warmer weather, indeed this summer it appears to have vanished completely.'

'Let us hope its absence continues,' he said.

'Indeed we must.'

'To make that happy sequel more likely, it's much to be desired that she goes somewhere more clement than England for the winter.'

'Yes, Malta seems for the moment to be the favourite, at your suggestion, I'm informed. As I said to the dear girl's aunt the other day, if she does go I'll consider very seriously a visit to Jamaica.'

'Your and my ancestral home.'

'Just so. And the seat of substantial business interests of mine, at which a closer look might be valuable.'

I was about to elaborate this point when it was borne in upon me that Kenyon was hardly listening. His attention seemed to have settled on something or someone at the far end of the gallery where we sat. What it was I could not see. Turning back to me he said, his kindly florid face showing animation,

'Elizabeth still receives letters from the poet Browning and exchanges letters with him.'

'So she does,' said I, somewhat amused at the confidence with which he made this statement.

'But when you and I last talked, you and he had yet to meet.'

'That is still a pleasure deferred.'

'It need be deferred no longer, I think, or perhaps only for a few more minutes. Robert Browning has this moment joined a small company up there. He's not the chap to stand on ceremony, and I've no doubt he would welcome the chance of making your acquaintance.'

'My dear Kenyon, I hardly feel—'

'Surely a golden opportunity, here on neutral ground.'

'I must ask you to excuse me. But I will, if I may, satisfy my curiosity about how the fellow looks. The cut of his jib, as I believe it's called. Which is he?'

'He's not in our view, but he took the chair nearest to the corner, facing this way. A small man, dark, impeccably dressed.'

Kenyon looked at me in some wonderment as I rose to my feet and strolled away along the gallery. I had very little idea of what had sent me on this slightly whimsical errand, until for a matter of a few seconds, and for the first and last time, I had sight of Robert Browning. His glance at me was brief, without hostility and without interest. Before I was past him his face grew lively at some remark from one of his party and he laughed and quickly answered. I moved on at the same pace and had soon completed the circuit back to my seat.

'You saw him, then?' asked Kenyon, alert for my answer.

'Yes. As clearly as I see you.'

'And you're satisfied he has no horns sprouting from his forehead.'

'Completely.'

'I'm glad to hear it. But he has a very dark complexion, didn't you think?'

'I suppose it might be called that.' Perhaps I spoke somewhat mechanically.

'So much so that I've heard it said he has Creole or coloured blood.'

'What an absurd suggestion.'

'Is it not, of one of the most cultivated men one is likely to meet? If required I could testify that, on the best authority, there's no truth in the tale. But, by an odd coincidence, it is true that Browning's family, like ours, has connections with the West Indies. More particularly, his paternal grandmother came from a family with extensive plantations and many slaves in St Kitts in the Leeward Islands, on the far side of the Caribbean. You must know that Browning senior, Robert's father, became a clerk at the Bank of England and is far from wealthy, though he seems content to support his son's poetry. The son and his sister grew up in New Cross, south of the . . . But whatever is the matter, my dear fellow? Are you unwell?'

'I beg your pardon,' I said as best I could. 'You're aware of my asthmatic tendency – I fear I'm suffering a mild attack, nothing for serious concern . . . perhaps the ventilation in this part of the building . . .'

'Of course we must get you home at once. I'll summon the porter and get him to go out and secure a cab to convey us.'

Over the next few days, giving out that I was indisposed, I kept to my room when at 50 Wimpole Street, leaving the house from time to time to make certain inquiries. At the end of this period, about the middle of the month, I went to Elizabeth's room about midday, having first made certain we should not be interrupted.

She greeted me amiably enough, though with something less than the warmth I had long grown to expect. 'Dearest papa! Are you quite recovered from your disorder?'

I thanked her for her solicitude, assured her I was myself again, and thereafter came straight to the point. 'I regret I must inform you, Elizabeth, that it will not after all be possible for you to spend the coming winter abroad.'

From her reception of that announcement, I could see easily enough that its drift came as no great surprise to her, though her disappointment was as evident. 'May I know your reason for this decree?'

'I am not bound to furnish a reason, but I will do so. My advice is that the discomfort and strain of the double journey would probably more than undo any beneficial effect of a few weeks in a warmer climate, not to speak of the various dangers attendant upon any foreign travel and sojourn.'

'I am willing to take that risk.'

'I am unwilling that a daughter of mine should do so.'

'I am of age, papa.'

'While you reside here and remain unmarried you will continue to be bound by your father's wishes.'

'Those conditions may not obtain for ever,' she said with a show of resolution.

'Indeed they may not. Is this a warning that they're about to end?'

She hesitated, then shook her head firmly but with despondency. 'No.'

'In that case I'll repeat that I sincerely wish things could have been otherwise touching your visit abroad, and I bid you good day.'

'Oh, papa.' With one of her nimble movements, Elizabeth barred my path to the door. 'Please, dear papa, will you not be open with me and tell me the whole truth?'

Now I hesitated. 'I very well remember,' I said, 'discussing with Mr Kenyon, your friend Mrs Jameson and yourself the possibility of your wintering on the Continent, this on more than one occasion, and your taking my side against the proposal, declaring you were just as well off in your own warm room, and the upheaval would not be worth while. Suddenly, the upheaval has become worth while. Why?'

She made no answer, but her cheeks flushed.

'When you're ready to answer that question,' I said as gently as I could, 'I will answer yours, and speak plain. I can only hope that day soon comes.'

I should never have given that promise. To keep it would have been to divulge my secret, and that I could never have done, not to Ba. Sometimes now I wish devoutly I could have brought myself to *speak plain*; more often I thank my stars I had the sense to keep my own counsel. But I must not indulge in idle fancies.

To my surprise, far from being dashed by my steadfast performance of my duty in at least forbidding her Continental visit, Elizabeth seemed cheerful and philosophical, content as always with being at home, surrounded by her family. That at any rate was what I told myself; I told myself many falsely comforting things. I find it almost impossible to believe that over all those months nothing of significance took place; nothing, that is, of which I was directly aware, except the abduction of Flush by ruffians and his eventual expensive recovery. The threatened loss of a dog! To be sure, I should have been greatly dashed if the attempt had succeeded, but there was a disparity between this and what I eventually did suffer so great as to be almost comical.

III

Early in the following August, everything changed, or rather, much was brought to light. I had found Robert Browning's continued regular visits to my daughter tolerable while they remained of specified duration. That day he overstayed his time and overstepped the mark. In a flash he shattered the protective shell in which I had encased myself. As soon as he had gone I hurried to Elizabeth's room in a towering rage, but the rage was directed inwards. No truer word was ever spoken than that there is none so blind as he who will not see.

Without preliminary I exclaimed, 'It appears, Ba, that *that man* has spent the whole day with you.'

'But papa, there was a storm, as surely you noticed. Mr Browning stayed only until the rain had stopped.'

'Confound the rain. To the devil with the rain. This reckless behaviour is insupportable. I will not have it. It must cease. Do you understand me?'

'I'm not sure,' said my daughter. 'Is it your meaning that Mr Browning is never to visit me here again?'

With renewed warmth, and no hesitation, I retorted, 'It is, it is. He is not to cross this threshold while I live, not for a hundred storms. He must never . . .'

'Dearest papa, you are overwrought. Come, let me sit you down here and make you see you're with one that loves you and will take care of you. Now what are these imaginings? For you seem to think Mr Browning is a sort of demon. Yet it's not so long since you seemed to tolerate his visits quite willingly and even, I thought, to welcome his addresses to me. Something has happened to change your mind. I beg you, tell your Ba what it is.'

'I cannot. Nothing has happened. But you are never to see that reprobate Browning again.'

'Mr Browning is an honourable English gentleman with none but the highest notions of what is right and proper. Or have you heard some lying tale to the contrary?'

'Nothing of that sort,' I had to answer. 'He is . . . he's simply not fit.'

'You refer presumably to his lack of a personal fortune.'

'You know there's very little that could be of less moment to me than any such consideration. In itself, that is. But the consequence of his lack of means must be that he lacks the sensibility required of him in his dealings with a personage such as yourself.'

'I can assure you that Mr Browning yields to no one where sensibility is concerned.'

'He attended no university.'

'His wealth of knowledge would challenge any who have. And since when was attendance of a university a guarantee of sensibility?'

'He is six years your junior.'

'Oh, stuff. Mama was four years older than you. Tell me the truth, father; why have you taken so strongly and so suddenly against poor Mr Browning? I remember so well how happy you were on my account when he first appeared.'

'That was before . . . . I will no longer permit his visits. Oh, Ba,' I burst out, 'pay heed to what I say as never before. I beg of you, be guided by me. I don't know what you and he are to each other, and I swear to you I don't wish to know, but let there be no more of it.' I stared at her and spoke with all the earnestness of which I am capable, 'In the name of God, my daughter, banish the man Robert Browning from your life.'

Truth is so terrible, even in fetters, that for a moment I thought I had won. Then Elizabeth turned away from me and said in level tones, 'I will not. Robert and I love each other. If God is to be brought into the matter, let Him part Robert and me, for nothing human will. If you try to prevent his entry into this house, I will leave it forthwith and trust to Mr Kenyon or Mr Boyd to help me. Now please go.'

So ended my last conversation with Elizabeth on this subject, in fact our last conversation worthy of the name in this world. On Saturday, 19th September, 1846, she left my house for ever, having a week earlier been married without my knowledge to Robert Browning at St Marylebone Parish Church. Soon the couple, taking Flush with them, were in Paris. Three weeks later they had reached Italy.

I suppose I had all along regarded it as inevitable, but to have such a thing happen, however clearly foreseen, is utterly different. But what else could I have done, knowing what I knew?

Let me set in order what I knew and if need be whence I knew and know it.

1. Robert Browning is of very dark complexion. (Kenyon's phrase; my own observation.)
2. It has been said in London that he is of Creole or coloured blood. (Kenyon.)
3. His ancestry includes a West Indian grandmother. (Kenyon.)
4. The style in which he expresses himself, while

correct grammatically, is fundamentally different from that of a true-born Englishman, not merely in his choice of words, but in his way of putting them together and their movement in his verses. (My own reading of the last-named and memory of what I heard of his first letter to Ba, also my glimpse of its cover.)

5. Mine is a slave-owning family domiciled in Jamaica for many years, indeed Elizabeth was the first for some generations to have been born in England.

6. I am myself of dark colouring.

7. Elizabeth is indeed of pale complexion, but there are distinct olive or sallow tints in that pallor. (Witness my personal pet-name for her.)

8. No West Indian person can be certain of his or her pedigree.

9. By a phenomenon known, I believe, as atavism, plants and animals have a tendency to reproduce earlier types. (My own observations in Jamaica.)

10. The laws of heredity are at present not well understood, but a child will often resemble its grandfather or grandmother rather than either of its immediate parents. (Common knowledge.)

It surely stands to reason and to common experience, requiring no further argument, that the presence of Creole blood on *both* sides of a union *must redouble to an incalculable degree the chances of Creole blood in the issue.*

No doubt in days to come the question of the colour of a human being's skin will seem no more and no less interesting than the colour of eyes or hair. Here in England in the reign of Queen Victoria, those days must appear impossibly far off. By the very same consideration, how could I tell my daughter that the combined heredities of herself and Browning might – very likely would not, but still *might* – produce black offspring? How could I go so far as to say I had a reason for trying to forbid their further association? The result must have been not only to destroy Ba's love for me, as the bearer of the worst of bad tidings, but also to place at risk her prospects of happiness. The latter I could not face. Better for all three concerned that I should continue to appear to my dearest Ba, and perhaps in time to the world, the very epitome of a selfish, obstinate, unreasoning tyrant. That is the part I must continue to play until my death. I resolve to do so and to keep my secret.

I pray that the Italians may be a more tolerant people in this regard than the English. They are after all a darker-skinned race than we.

Wimpole Street,
October, 1846

IV

Until now I have resisted all temptations to add to the foregoing. I subjoined not a word even on that blackest day in November, 1850 when Elizabeth's *Poems* in two volumes appeared in a new edition that contained a section entitled *Sonnets from the Portuguese*, evidently addressed to the man now her husband. I could bring myself to do no more than hastily glance through these poems; they seemed to me of a most improper, indeed disgusting intimacy, but it was not that which wounded my feelings. The title is intended to puzzle or misdirect the reader, but if it had been specifically meant to cause me pain it could not have been more artfully devised. For 'little Portuguese' was my own personal pet-name for her, kept a secret between the two of us, an affectionately teasing allusion to her pale honey-coloured skin. The thought of her violation of this precious confidence, of my name for her being, so to speak, filched away and handed to a man who, whatever else may be said of him, had known her for only five of her forty-four years – there are no fitting words. The first shock brought a return of the asthma from which I had suffered earlier in the year, and even now the hurt remains keen.

But for the moment, in the face of a second, graver blow, I am incapable of such Stoical forbearance. Yesterday I was in my dining room at 50 Wimpole Street when I heard from the hall the unmistakable sound of a child's laughter and screams of delight. These were noises quite foreign to my house. I at once connected them with the known presence in London, not merely of my estranged daughter and her husband on their third visit, but of their six-year-old son, the child whose very existence I had tried to efface from my mind. Knowing what I must do, I inhaled several deep breaths; then, willing my head not to renew its trembling, I opened the dining-room door and strode into the hall.

There, on all fours in imitation of a lion or some such beast, was my son George Moulton-Barrett, and, retreating from him in feigned alarm, there was my grandson, Robert Wiedemann Browning. We stared at each other for what seemed an eternity, but was probably no more than two minutes. I could think of nothing to say and doubt whether, in any case, I could have spoken a word. The little lad facing me, whose looks reminded me strongly of my dead son Edward's, could have served as artist's model for a picture of a typical English boy, with the unambiguous fair colouring that that implies.

At last I turned and went back into the dining room, having mastered my strong desire to pick the youngster up and hug him to my breast. When I was breathing more or less normally I summoned George there. He stood before me, serious, dependable, the one of my sons I most respected.

'Whose child is that, George?' I asked, still not finding speech easy.

'Ba's child, father,' he answered.

'And what is he doing here, pray?'

'He is waiting, sir, waiting until it's time to return to his mother. I mean to take him on the short journey in a few moments. Would you come with us?'

'I fear not, George. Truly I cannot.'

'Papa, I beg of you. It would make Ba so happy.'

'No, my boy. Leave me. And kindly remove the child forthwith.'

When I heard the front door shut after the two, I lowered my head into my hands and may possibly have shed a tear. So it had all been for nothing, I said to myself. What I had taken for facts had not all been facts, that or my conclusions from them had been erroneous. But if I truly thought I had been wrong, why had I refused to go to Ba with George and her son?

After a troubled night, I awoke this morning with the answer rising to my lips. My daughter is now forty-nine years old and some months. In the nature of things, it must be unlikely that she could bear another child, so unlikely that I can rule it out, feel untroubled by any possibility. But I find I still cannot bring myself to come face to face with her, and with *him*. I could bear her silent reproaches, his silent triumph, but not their pity. *Her* pity.

Wimpole Street,
August, 1855

V

The above is of course fiction, but it contains much fact, the prime example being Mr Barrett's ten points.

With the exception of (4), all are matters of record. (9) and (10) certainly hold for the mid-nineteenth century, and I was told of (8) by a Jamaican friend in the 1970s. As regards (4), Mr Barrett had undoubtedly seen something in Browning's work which many would agree was there without thinking it the result of being an untrue-born Englishman. Further, it might be instructive to produce suitably recondite but representative extracts from Browning and, say, Wordsworth, Leigh Hunt, Byron, Keats, Hood, Beddoes, Tennyson, Clough and Arnold, and present them blind to a good class with the instruction to pick out which one was the work of a West Indian. The Browning sample might be the following excerpt from 'Nationality in Drinks', which Mr Barrett could easily have read, since it was first collected in *Dramatic Romances and Lyrics* in 1845:

Up jumped Tokay on our table,
Like a pygmy castle-warder,
Dwarfish to see, but stout and able,
Arms and accoutrements all in order;
And fierce he looked North, then, wheeling South,
Blew with his bugle a challenge to Drouth,
Cocked his flap-hat with the tosspot-feather,
Twisted his thumb in his red moustache,
Jingled his huge brass spurs together,
Tightened his waist with its Buda sash,
And then, with an impudence nought could abash,
Shrugged his hump-shoulder, to tell the beholder,
For twenty such knaves he should laugh but the bolder;
And so, with his sword-hilt gallantly jutting,

> *And dexter-hand on his haunch abutting,*
> *Went the little man, Sir Ausbruch, strutting!*

Other facts in my story include Browning's first letter to Elizabeth and the extracts from it; the paraphrase of her reply; Mr Barrett's membership of the Reform Club; his asthmatic weakness, including the severe attack of 1850; Browning's visit in August, 1846 and the reason offered for its prolongation; and Mr Barrett's meeting with his grandson. 'The Portuguese' was certainly Browning's pet-name for Elizabeth; there is no evidence it was ever her father's.

With one exception, I mean the thoughts and feelings I attribute to Mr Barrett to be sincere on his part, truthful. The exception is his final paragraph, where his explanation for not wanting to face Elizabeth and Browning strikes me as distinctly thin. His 'real' motive is more likely to have been fear of betraying his jealousy at seeing the two unequivocally together, with their offspring. (Not a sexual jealousy: I have never believed that he harboured a guilty passion for his daughter.) And perhaps he was still obsessed by his theory. Anyhow, he died in 1857 at the age of seventy-two; Elizabeth survived him by only four years.

I myself think it most unlikely that Browning, any more than Elizabeth, had some 'Creole' blood, though, if he had had, Victorian literature and the world in general would be that much more interesting. He would have been the English member of a great trio of European coloured writers of the nineteenth century, the other being Alexander Dumas père (black grandmother) and Alexander Pushkin (black great-grandfather), both of whom can be taken as sharing something of his spirit.

A few additional facts may be of interest. In 1972 I gave a talk on Tennyson to a literary society in Barnet. I was glad that what I had to say was entirely favourable to the poet, because my audience included his highly articulate ninety-three-year-old grandson, Sir Charles Tennyson (1879–1977), though that is by the way. In the closing stages of the meeting, the secretary of the society took me aside.

'Now I know Tennyson wasn't the same person as Browning, but we have a Mrs [I forget] in the audience, a descendant of Browning's brother. Would you like a word with her?'

'Very much,' I said.

The word I had with the lady was not memorable, but I was most interested to find she was black, especially when I checked afterwards and found that Browning had no brother. None known to history, that is.

Boris and the Colonel

I

Edward Saxton was the Fellow and Director of Studies in English at a small Cambridge college, and concurrently a lecturer in that subject at that university. His special interest, on which he had given a course for over fifteen years, was the work of Thomas Gray, William Collins, Oliver Goldsmith and lesser poets of the eighteenth century who were then collectively regarded as precursors of the Romantic movement. The events recounted here took place in 1962, when Edward was forty-five years old; a thin, rather tall figure with a perceptible stoop.

He still lived where he had done when his wife had died suddenly two years earlier, in what called itself an old mill house in a village some miles east of Cambridge. He had a green shooting-brake and used it to drive himself to and fro most days during term. One such day in late spring found him in the college room he used for teaching, a few minutes before his first pupil was due.

This pupil was unlike his others in more than one way. To begin with it was a girl he expected, an undergraduate at one of the women's colleges. Also unusually, she was so interested in her subject that, over and above a weekly tutorial hour with her own Director of Studies, she had come to an arrangement whereby she showed her work to Edward four times a term. This was due partly to his personal qualities and partly to her third point of singularity, a family connection with him.

Lucy Masterman was a niece of Louise, Edward's dead wife, child of her elder brother, now in her second year at the university and nearly twenty years old. She was sturdy, dark-haired, rosy-cheeked, with large watchful brown eyes, a feature she had shared with Louise. She still retained the artless manner she had shown as a little girl, though Edward had sometimes thought she found it came in handy when dealing with grey-haired scholars like himself.

That manner was in place when, punctual as ever, she arrived. Indeed, that morning it was slightly more marked than usual, if anything, but when he looked back afterwards it seemed no time at all before Lucy was reading him her essay, and scarcely longer till she was illustrating her set theme, 'Gray's use of the rhymed quatrain in his *Elegy*'.

> *Far from the madding crowd's ignoble strife* (she read)
> *Their sober wishes never learned to stray;*
> *Along the cool sequestered vale of life*
> *They kept the noiseless tenor of their way.*

Lucy's comment was that the simple inhabitants of Gray's village might have been surprised to receive such a weighty tribute, with its heavy, regular rhythms and its tendency to epigram. A stanza such as the following, she went on, might have sounded more comfortable and comprehensible:

> *But if one should return whose errant mind* (she read)
> *From rustic toil once took him far abroad,*
> *All then would labour merely to be kind,*
> *And crave his presence at their humble board.*

The excitement that filled Edward on hearing these

last four lines was quite unfamiliar to him, and it was not paralleled by anything that happened later. It had reached its full strength almost at once, and he could not remember afterwards how he had restrained himself from giving way to his feelings. For a moment he was young again, when anything had seemed possible. As Lucy paused, he asked her to stop for a minute in tones suited to a real command, and in an uncharacteristic movement got up and paced the floor.

'Did you know, Lucy,' he said in his diffident tenor, when nearly half that minute had passed and he was himself again, 'that that stanza appears nowhere in any received text of the *Elegy*?'

She blushed easily, as he had noticed. She did so now. 'I thought it might be a cancelled stanza from one of the extant manuscripts.'

'The so-called Eton manuscript has seven such stanzas, none of which even approximately resembles in any way the four lines you have just read me.'

Her blush deepened but she said nothing.

'In any case Gray would never have written those lines,' he pursued.

'You seem very sure.'

'So would you be, my dear, if you were once to hear in them what I heard. Read them aloud again.' As soon as she had finished, Edward said, 'There. Does that sound all right to you?'

'Well . . .'

'What about the rhymes?'

She looked at her page again and this time noticed something. 'Oh.'

'Precisely. *Mind* and *kind* are perfectly acceptable, if a little trite. *Abroad* and *board*, despite the words' similarity to the eye, are not acceptable, as any speaker from the west of England or Ireland or America outside the South

27

would spot immediately.' If Edward's habitual manner had anything vague or preoccupied in it, there was nothing of either to be seen in him by this time.

Lucy perhaps saw this. She said tentatively, '*Abroad* rhymes with *Claude* and *Maud*, and . . .'

'And *fraud*. And *board* with *abhorred* and *harpsichord* and what you will. No poet of the eighteenth century, certainly not one as fastidious and well educated as Gray, could even have contemplated such a false equivalence.'

'So my sententious quatrain is a fake.'

'I'm afraid so. The work of a contemporary speaker of standard English, at a guess, possessing a good but not intimate knowledge of English poetry of the period, and more certainly a defective ear. Now. To begin with, not your work, Lucy.'

'No. I found it in a cupboard in one of the guest bedrooms at home among some sheets of typing paper, which was what I'd really been after, the typing paper. I'd come across it there ages before and I'd just left it and forgotten about it until I needed some, some typing paper. You know how you do. And it was just there in with the other sheets, the sheet with that stanza typed on it.'

'But who'd typed it, who'd written it, have you any idea?'

'Not really. Some guest, I suppose. I'm often not there, you know, at home. Most of the time, in fact.'

'Can I see it, the paper you found?'

Lucy hesitated. 'I chucked it away. Probably somebody going in for one of those weekend competitions in the *New Statesman* or somewhere. You know – write some lines in the manner of this or that well-known poem.'

'Very likely.' This explanation, like the rest of Lucy's last couple of remarks, did not satisfy Edward, but the light fog of boredom in which he habitually lived had begun to seep back in, and for the moment he could not understand or quite believe in the animation of his first response to what now seemed four rather ordinary lines. 'But . . . what made you put it into your essay like that, in a way that suggested as strongly as possible that it was a bona fide part of Gray's poem?'

'Oh, that was just rather silly.' Lucy showed some discomfort at being asked such a question. 'I was wondering if you'd spot it, but I knew you would and of course you did as soon as I finished reading it, didn't you?'

'Almost. But I still don't quite see what you hoped to gain from your little deception.'

'Nothing at all. It was just a joke.'

Edward's response to this information suggested he was no stranger to jokes, but had got out of the habit of responding to them. Perhaps he had come to find it an effort to laugh. 'I thought as much,' he said, laughing now. 'But it seems to have recoiled on your own head, Lucy dear.'

'What? Oh, I see. Yes, I suppose it has a bit. In a way.'

'Well, I think we might get on with things, don't you?'

And in no time she was citing the carrying-over of the sense between the sixteenth and seventeenth stanzas as the only case in the entire poem, and pronouncing on the significance of that. It was a well-written essay, one that showed some real feeling for literature, as Lucy's always were and always did. When she had finished reading it and discussing it and its subject with Edward, they agreed that for next time she should consider the justice of Johnson's remark, 'In all Gray's odes there is a kind of cumbrous splendour which we wish away.'

She was rising to go when Edward said to her, 'Have you really no notion at all who it was that put together that piece of pseudo-*Elegy* you found?'

'None whatever, I'm afraid. As I said, I'm not usually there.'

'It might have been interesting to know.'

The matter was left at that for the time being.

Some weeks later, Edward was sitting in the common room of his college drinking a glass of sherry before dinner. He regularly did so whenever he dined in college, and he did that most nights, not because he particularly enjoyed either the fare or the company but because he preferred them to the alternative, a solitary meal prepared by himself in his kitchen at the old mill house. He was on visiting terms with several married couples both in Cambridge itself and in the country outside, but he was not the kind of man to attract or to welcome any kind of regular arrangement for getting himself fed by friends. Now and then he dined out in another college, and once or twice a term he spent the weekend at the house of his brother-in-law, but the evening in question was what his evenings generally were.

The presence in the armchair next to his of Roger Ashby, the Fellow in Modern European History, had over some years become an expected part of those evenings. Edward had no objection, except when Ashby commented on what he saw as the similarity of their situations, having divorced his wife four years previously and not remarried. This proved not to be one of those occasions. Instead, so to speak, he asked in a meaning tone if Edward had seen the newspaper that day.

'Not yet,' said Edward. He had explained more than once to Ashby that he held off doing so until the time of his final snack and his nightcap at home.

'Thing in it that's bound to interest you. A fellow claims to have discovered some previously unknown lines from Gray's *Elegy*. Which if I mistake not is a poem that lies within your field, my dear fellow-toiler?'

'Very much so. Does the paper quote the passage in question?'

'Yes, but I fear . . . Ah. Excuse me.'

While Ashby crossed the room and returned to his seat, Edward felt in himself an onset of that same excitement that had visited him when Lucy started to recite her spurious stanza. Now as then, he found it hard to sit still.

'Yes,' said Ashby, turning to the middle pages of the captured newspaper and clearly preparing to read the relevant part aloud.

Edward forestalled that by saying, 'Let me see if I already know how those lines run.'

'I thought you said you hadn't yet—'

'Nevertheless, I have a feeling I may know them. You can hear me if you would.'

Ashby gave in with a fairly good grace, and said nothing while Edward recited verbatim what he had heard from Lucy at that tutorial. This feat of memory drew no appreciation from Ashby, who kept his eyes on what was before them and moved his head tentatively in small lateral jerks. 'Is that all?' he asked finally.

'Yes. Am I right?'

After a headshake of greater amplitude than before, Ashby said, 'Well, it might be best if I simply read you what's here.'

'I'd sooner see it with my own eyes,' said Edward. He had a well-founded distrust of the other man's willingness or ability to read anything aloud without oral annotations of his own. The words on the page proved to be set out in a way that obscured their function as part of a stanzaic scheme, but he soon rectified that in his mind and read:

> *Should one retrace his steps whose foolish dream*
> *From righteous labours lured him far astray,*
> *None but would hail him as he drove his team,*
> *And court his company at close of day.*
>
> *Secure all night within his peasant cot,*
> *Each morn he treads the land that gave him birth,*
> *And contemplates some not unhonoured spot*
> *To house his weary bones in native earth.*

Edward had fully taken in these lines before it occurred to him to do as much as glance at the surrounding matter. This informed him that the two stanzas quoted had come to light among a packet of manuscript papers in the library of a London house whose name meant nothing to him. The authenticity of the documents was uncertain, but was being checked by experts in eighteenth-century literature and in the history of writing materials. The finder of the papers wished to remain anonymous while verification was still proceeding, but was himself a well-known authority on the poetry of the period.

Some minutes had gone by since Edward had begun to read, a longer interval than Ashby normally let pass in silence. He turned out to be on his way back from the buttery hatch carrying two glasses of sherry, and soon overrode Edward's protest that a single drink before Hall was as much as he allowed himself.

'Have you formed any opinion on the authenticity of those verses?' asked Ashby.

'My first tentative impression,' said Edward carefully, 'is that their author is unlikely to have been Thomas Gray.' His mind was still perturbed at this unlooked-for sequel to the Lucy stanza, as he called it to himself, and what it might mean.

'You are clearly not one of the experts consulted by the

anonymous finder. Which is a little surprising, isn't it? Given your well-known eminence.'

'Thank you, Roger, but there are quite a few others of at least equal eminence.'

'Really. Perhaps less ready than you to detect a forgery.'

'That's possible too, of course.'

'Whereas a successful forgery would be worth a great deal of money.'

'These days a reasonably careful and physically prepossessing forgery of such a famous poem, even if openly acknowledged to be a forgery, would be worth a substantial sum, especially in America. It would be interesting to have a look at that manuscript. I wonder whether—'

What Edward wondered competed unsuccessfully with the buzzing of the internal telephone. Answering this was something Ashby seemed to like doing. He threaded his way across the room between couples of old dons and young dons and a parson or two and spoke into the instrument. When he hung up his eyes were on Edward.

'Call from Suffolk for you in the lodge,' said Ashby. 'A Miss Masterman.'

Edward was picking up the receiver in the porter's lodge in much less time than he had taken over the newspaper. He was breathing quite fast as he gave his name.

'This is your favourite pupil and relative,' said the familiar youthful voice. 'How are you?'

'Fine, but why aren't you in Cambridge?'

'Revising for exams, of course. You could give me a tip or two there, especially over the Metaphysicals. It's been simply ages since we saw you down this way. I was just thinking, if you happen to be free, why don't you turn up at your usual time on Friday?'

'My dear Lucy, I can't think of anything I'd rather do.'

The warmth of Edward's response was clearly a little surprising to Lucy. 'Oh,' she said. 'Well, that is good news, I must say. I'm afraid it'll be deadly dull, just me and the aged parents.'

'Couldn't be better.'

'Couldn't it? I was going to offer an inducement, but it seems you don't need one.'

'What sort of inducement?'

'Just, there's a bit more to tell you about, you remember, that Gray's *Elegy* thing. You know, that cod verse I stuck in my essay.'

He very nearly screeched at her to tell him instantly, but thought he had better refrain in the circumstances. Instead, he asked her, 'You've seen the paper today, have you?'

'Well yes, but what about it?'

'Look again. Page 7.'

'A second and more successful attempt, or at least a subsequent one.'

Lucy had settled herself on the floor of her parents' drawing room in one of those squatting attitudes impossible for any normal male west of Suez. 'Are we sure about that? If it matters, that is.'

'That sort of thing always matters,' said Edward from the sofa. 'No, we're not sure, how could we ever be, but there's a strong suggestion in the fact that this time he avoids the cockney rhyme we noticed in your text. Presumably he noticed it too. Could I have another look at what you've shown me?'

'My text, golly!' said Lucy, passing him the type-written sheet.

'M'm. Yes, this is a workpaper all right, leading to fair copy, probably with one or two precursors. Earlier efforts to you.'

'Thank you, Uncle.'

'How certain are you that there are no other bits hanging about somewhere?'

'As certain as I can be without taking the bloody place apart brick by brick.'

'All right, Lucy. Well, there it is. I'd give a lot to know who it was that cooked up this stuff.'

'Would you? What would you do if you did know? What good would it do you?'

'Put it down to interest. Or instinct. I just want to know.'

'Would it help to know who typed what you've got there?'

'What are you talking about, of course it would. A hundred, a thousand to one they're the same person. Why? Surely you're not going to tell me you know who it was? I don't think I could stand another shock.'

Lucy jumped up from the rug and seated herself next to Edward, turning her top half round towards him in her best unselfconscious style. 'I'm afraid I have been rather saving this up to tell you face to face.'

'Like the typescript. All right, but please keep it as short as you can.'

'Of course, what do you take me for? The first thing was me tracing the typewriter. That was easy.'

She brought out a sheet that, while a little crumpled, resembled in its general appearance the one he already held. Edward compared them.

'The typings are certainly very similar,' he said after a minute or two.

'More than just very similar. Look at the "d" in *mind* and *abroad* and so on. The bulgy part has got a little break in it near the bottom. You see? And the "s" all over the place, too far over to the right. And the "h". Almost like an "n".'

After a shorter interval, Edward said, 'Yes, I do see. But what . . .'

'It belongs to my dad. As soon as I saw it, the original one, I thought I knew it. Somebody staying here for the weekend borrowed it off him one afternoon. Would you like to know who it was?'

'Oh, I suppose I might as well, now we've come this far.'

'Good. He's called Colonel Orion Procope.' She spelt the surname. 'Three syllables, stress on first,' she explained. 'Strikes a chord?'

'There's a restaurant in Paris called something analogous, but I'm afraid I've never heard of any such person.'

'I've an idea there's a Sir in front of most of that or perhaps a Lord hanging about somewhere, and I'm pretty sure there's an MC after it. Evidently he did something jolly gallant in the desert. Any better?'

'Sorry.'

'Well, I had a shot, at least. Mind you, the colonel, which is how he likes to be addressed – Colonel Orion Procope has rather got the look of, you know, someone who changes his name about a bit. Anyway, you'll have the chance of judging such things for yourself in a little while.'

'What!'

'My turn to be sorry,' said Lucy, neither sounding nor looking particularly sorry. 'Yes, he's coming to dinner. I promise that's the last of my surprises.'

'For this weekend at least. Well, that's a comfort.'

Before they went off to change, Lucy released some further crumbs of information about the gallant colonel. He lived no great distance away, across Suffolk, near the coast; having never married, he lived there on his own, 'apart no doubt from the occasional fisherman', according to Lucy; he got invited over for the weekend a couple of times a year, for dinner or Sunday lunch two or three times as often; he might never have been invited at all but for his apparently lonely situation, 'and he most likely wouldn't have been even so, if Mum weren't such an old softie'; he had first met Lucy's father in the course of some 'strangulatingly boring' piece of business in the City of London; he had never been known to say much about his history.

Edward had his usual room at the eastern end of the house, usual at least since Louise's death. For some months after that death, he had thought he would never have been able to come down here again, but when once he decided to try, it had not proved so difficult. These days, in fact, the place was only fitfully one where he had known some happy moments with her; he valued it more for itself, for its spaciousness, though it was not very grand or very old, and its silence. He liked this part of East Anglia too, never sunny for long, but at some time every day full of light from its enormous sky, which Constable had never forgotten.

Of course this was Lucy's place too. Now that she was momentarily out of his sight, he found it easier to think of her as an entire person, easier too to consider with some objectivity her resemblances to her aunt, seen in her colouring and the look of her face with its round eyes and arched brows, and felt rather than seen in the way she held herself, upright but with head a little bowed. He now doubted the truth of his earlier impression that the glance of those brown eyes had grown more direct recently. But was he accurate in supposing that he saw her first of all as a version of Louise?

He was tying his tie at the dressing table when out of the tail of his eye he caught a distant movement through the east window. He soon saw a car descending a low hill

37

in the nearer distance. For a few seconds it vanished before reappearing and entering the short driveway, an expensive-looking car sprayed a very dark blue picked out with crimson. After it drew up, just beyond rather than below where Edward was standing, nothing happened for a short time. Then a youngish man in a dark suit and a chauffeur's cap got out of the driving seat and another about Edward's age out of the passenger's seat. What could be seen of the latter showed him to be an average sort of man in a dinner jacket, not tall, not short, with a mop of brown hair that seemed to have kept most of its colour, but there was something about the presumable Colonel Procope that made Edward draw cautiously back from his window.

There was no trace of that something to be seen when in due course the two men met. Indeed, the colonel made a favourable impression with his generally straightforward manner and the restrained warmth with which he greeted the three Mastermans. When he came to Edward, he managed to convey satisfaction at meeting one he had heard good reports of. He was quite unmilitary in his appearance, which by including a remnant of stubble by one ear and a loosely tied tie rather suggested some colleague of Edward's, or the popular idea of one. It might perhaps have been said that he talked a little too quietly for perfect manners.

The first patch of conversation that Edward remembered afterwards came during dinner, and was preceded by a brief warning look, or glare, at him from Lucy.

'Oh, colonel,' she said, 'I am right in thinking, am I not, that you got a medal for something brave you did in the war?'

Before answering, Procope moved his eyes to her and only then turned his head, a slightly disconcerting trick Edward had noticed in him before. 'A medal?' he echoed with humorous pomposity. 'Come, every Tom, Dick and Harry gets a medal. What they gave me was a decoration, what? The old MC, you know. In fact, Lucy girl, you know perfectly well.'

'I wanted to be sure because one of my college mates I happened to be telling about you said she was pretty sure she remembered her father saying he'd known somebody with your name or something like it in the war in North Africa somewhere.'

'When you've got your breath back, tell me what unit he was in.' The colonel made a vaguely conspiratorial face at Lucy's mother, Kate Masterman, who beamed back at him. The two were certainly on good terms, Edward thought, but in no more than a companionable way, without any trace on Kate's side of the old softie of her daughter's description.

Lucy seemed to search her memory. 'Could he have been a Desert Rat?'

'Certainly he could. I had very little to do with them. They were strictly the Seventh Armoured; I was with the Tenth. Most of the time.'

'Of course, Edward was in the desert too, weren't you, uncle?'

'Only for a couple of weeks,' said Edward discouragingly. He had seen his share of action, but had got no nearer 'the desert' than Anzio in Italy.

If Lucy had hoped to drive Procope into some sort of corner, to force him into undue reticence or talkativeness, she was disappointed. In five minutes or so he had shown that he had either experienced fighting in North Africa at first hand or been thoroughly briefed by somebody who had. Whichever it was, Edward could see nothing at all in him of any kind of man that might have tried to fake a couple of Gray's *Elegy* quatrains. On the other hand, it had to be conceded that he did look a bit like one given to changing his name about, as Lucy had put it. Edward felt this strongly enough to see something false in the chummy au revoir the fellow sent Kate when the two women left the table.

So, what with one thing and another, Edward was more than adequately surprised to hear Procope say, almost as soon as the door was shut, 'I gather you're a great authority on Thomas Gray, Dr Saxton. The chap who wrote the *Elegy*.'

'I suppose one might put it like that. Nice of you to anyhow, colonel.'

Procope made one of his faces. 'Well, it's true. Now you obviously think Gray's pretty good as a poet, otherwise you wouldn't have bothered to turn yourself into an authority on him.'

'Yes, at least pretty good.'

'Sorry. Of course, I know I'm a complete what-you-may-call-it, a layman, an amateur, but I've always been fond of the old hoary-headed swain and the rest of it. Time was when I could have repeated whole chunks that I'd got by heart. Don't you worry, Toby, I'm not about to start polluting your dining room with a poetry recital.'

Toby Masterman made some inoffensive remark. To Edward's eyes he looked indisputably more like a military man than his guest, but like nothing positive that could be thought of, stout, almost florid, unlike his dead sister with a completeness once mildly comic to Edward and now the cause of mild thankfulness. The only surprising thing about him was that he had produced Lucy.

After a laudatory word or two about the port now in circulation, Procope said with renewed vivacity, 'Things being as they are, I consider myself lucky to have run across an expert like you, Dr Saxton, just when there's been this thing in the paper about some extra verses of the poem seeming to have turned up from somewhere. You must have seen that, naturally. Tell me, off the record, so to speak, what did you think of them, those verses? I quite see you may prefer not to commit yourself until you know more about the thing.'

Edward tried to remember that the question had come from the apparent author of the verses in question. 'Well,' he said cautiously, 'as regards poetical merit, what I saw struck me as distinctly below par, below the general standard of the *Elegy*, but then what Gray wrote is so familiar that one can't be sure. What I'm trying to say is, it's hard to compare the known with the unknown.'

'I'm pretty hopeless myself when it comes to anything like that. But I value your opinion, welcome it too, because it throws some light on a question I have to admit interests me more, the authenticity of those eight lines. Taking into account your first reaction to them as poetry, do you think they're Gray's work or not? As far as you can tell.'

This seemed to Edward one to fend off. 'That's more difficult,' he said. 'Not really one for me at all. I don't know enough about Gray's lesser contemporaries to be sure.'

'You're too modest, Dr Saxton. You must have some feeling one way or the other.'

'I wouldn't like to commit myself to any such feeling without looking at the stuff again.'

'That's easily arranged.' Procope brought out a wallet from which he carefully took a neat newspaper cutting. 'It just so happens, as they say.'

Edward tried to feign a pleased interest as he looked again at what Roger Ashby had shown him earlier that week. He felt himself blushing to a degree that might have rivalled Lucy, and did his best to put on a fit of coughing. It was extraordinarily hard to read the printed words as opposed to looking in their general direction.

'I'm sorry, Toby,' said Procope, 'we'll be finished in a minute.'

'Take your time, I'm quite comfortable as I am.'

'You saw the piece, did you? What do you think?'

'I think the port is with you,' said Toby.

Possibly because he was seeing the stanzas in changed circumstances, Edward all at once found in them something he had not noticed before, something that brought on in him a more intense agony of dissimulation. He decided he had to speak and might as well speak the truth.

'In my opinion these lines are not the work of Thomas Gray,' he said.

'Ah! Thank you! Thank you, Dr Saxton, for delivering the kind of verdict that I slightly hoped you would see your way to.'

Instead of frankly goggling at the colonel, Edward tried to look no more than politely interested and expectant.

'As I told you just now, I'm a total amateur in literary matters, interested as I may be in one or two of them, but even so, or perhaps for that very reason, I find it pleasant when a professional confirms my subjective judgement.'

This time Edward managed to say, 'Yes, I see.'

'I take it you've been approached by whoever's concerned and asked for your expert opinion? No? Well, they'll come to you, never fear. When they do, I hope you'll denounce this impudent fabrication. As before, that's only a, what did I say, a slight hope of mine, a modest one. Because, although the matter has aroused my curiosity, it matters to me personally not at all whether those lines are genuine or spurious. Not one scrap. I haven't even taken a bet. What do you say to that, Toby?'

'I say we should consider joining the ladies.'

When the colonel had departed and Lucy slipped away to bed, Edward forgathered with Toby and Kate for a nightcap in a corner of the drawing room. Outside the house the stillness seemed absolute.

'Interesting sort of chap, Colonel Procope,' said Edward experimentally.

The experiment was not a success. Kate said she thought the colonel was rather pathetic, Toby said more apologetically that neighbours had become thin on the ground, and the topic lapsed before Edward could get out his prepared quip about the fellow reminding him of some dishonest smallholder. A moment later Kate asked Edward how he thought Lucy was looking, at which point Toby shifted in his chair in a way suggesting that there had been enough recent discussion of his daughter to last him for a bit.

This time Edward spoke guardedly. 'She looks fine to me,' he said, and was not surprised to hear from Kate that mere outward looks were a trifle compared with inner wellbeing or the lack of it, and that it was here that Lucy gave grounds for concern, having just broken suddenly with an altogether suitable near-fiancé.

'About nothing at all,' said Kate. 'All of a sudden he became a frightful bore.'

'For my money he'd been that all along,' said Toby. 'Full of, well, full of what there was of himself. Damn it, the girl must be allowed to make a mistake and change her mind now and then. She's not twenty yet.'

'It's much more than that, as you know. She's thoroughly discontented with her whole generation of young men and always has been. You'd have thought Cambridge would have opened her eyes, but from that point of view it's been a total washout.'

'Oh, Katie, give the poor little thing a chance. She needs time.'

'If there's anything I can do,' said Edward.

'It's sweet of you, dear Edward, but I get the impression that where that girl's concerned you're impossibly distant and grown-up. Oh, she's very fond of you, of course, so she ought to be, but as a remote sort of uncle-figure, which after all is what you are. You do enough for her by encouraging her interest in literature.'

And that ought to be enough for any uncle-figure, thought Edward a little later as he undressed in his single bedroom. He switched off his light and looked out over the soundless landscape. In a corner of his mind were an excitement and something to be looked forward to with a tiny thrill. The excitement was from Gray and Procope, the something was the prospect of conferring again with Lucy. But a thrill of any size that arose from that prospect could be no more than a function of habit and memory.

'And I'm quite sure he meant it,' Edward told Lucy the next morning, by way of winding up his account of the conversation with Colonel Procope.

'But he can't have,' she said.

'On one assumption, it would indeed be all one to the colonel whether those stanzas are genuine or not. It would not concern him either which they are shown or taken to be. Let's see if you can find grounds for . . .'

He stopped speaking because she seemed to have stopped listening. They had reached the gate of the small paddock, which they now entered. Lucy clinked the handle of the pail she was carrying, not loudly but it appeared loudly enough to attract the attention of a large horse standing by the far hedge. This animal at once came trotting over to them with what to Edward was excessive eagerness. Seen close to, it looked about the size of a full-grown elk, reddish-brown in general colour but with black mane and tail and large off-white teeth. These it showed prominently while it breathed noisily at them, butted Edward in the chest and without ceremony set about bolting the contents of the pail.

'You remember Boris,' said Lucy and, when Edward looked uncomprehending, added a trifle impatiently. 'You know, after Boris Godunov.'

'I thought it was Virginia, after Virginia Woolf.'

'That was the little mare I had ages ago. She's gone. It's Boris now.'

Indeed it was Boris now, in the extra sense that Lucy's attention was all directed that way, with none to spare for Edward. Presently she threw a rope round the horse's neck and in a flash was on its back. For a moment she sat there very still and straight and seeming taller than before; Edward almost caught his breath at her look of dignity and power. Then she was off, away, just a girl trotting and cantering her horse round her father's paddock. He, Toby, had prophesied that the horse would be disposed of about the time she found herself a man.

As soon as he profitably could, the man she was with at the moment said, 'Now, Lucy, I want you to do a little experiment for me.' While she shut the gate behind them he took out his copy of the stanzas, but did not at once hand it over. 'Try to forget that this might or might not be part of Gray's *Elegy*. See if you can manage to forget the fact that it's in verse, which shouldn't be all that exacting considering the lubberly way the paper has set it out. Now. You've no idea what this might be, you've just this moment come across it written on a pad. Right, here it is.'

Lucy halted on the gravel drive to read. He thought it

marvellous that she found no evident difficulty in doing so without artificial aid and in what was not much better than average daylight, living as he did in a world where everybody wore glasses, most of them all the time, like himself. In his eagerness he tried to prompt her by suggesting she should attend only to the meaning of what was in front of her, but she spoke at the same time, and with a shake of the head at his own ineptitude he told her to go on.

'What it *says* . . . if somebody who went wrong or went to ,the wrong place should retrace his steps, come back to his starting-point, he'd be perfectly . . .'

'Secure. The best word out of however many dozen it is. Though not at all Gray's kind of thing, a sort of pun, Latin *securus*, *se* plus *cura*, free from care, also modern *secure*, in a state of security, not at risk from hostile undercover moves or surveillance.'

'In fact the message of the whole thing seems to be . . .'

Edward was too excited to notice that he had again interrupted. 'The message. That's what it is. A message. Well done. It suddenly hit me last night. What is the characteristic of that newspaper and no other, almost no other anywhere? All right, there are several, but the one that interests us is that it goes all over the world.'

'*Far* astray.'

'If you wanted to send a message to somebody you couldn't locate, perhaps you couldn't even say with any certainty what country he was in, what better means could you think of? Almost, what other means at all? Exposed as a forgery or not, you really could afford to be indifferent. You might even leave drafts of it lying about.'

'Provided your man saw it.'

'Admittedly you'd have to take your chance on that,

but you might be able to bet he'd see that paper every day. Of course he'd have to have some sort of interest in literature thrown in, but with a thing like the *Elegy* it wouldn't have to be a specialised one. And if there's silence at the other end you just have to think of something else. You're no worse off.'

They had reached the road before Lucy said, 'All right, let's have the rest of it, whatever it is.'

'How do you know there's more to come?'

'By not being blind or deaf. Come on, Uncle – shoot.'

'Very well, here goes. One. Colonel Orion Procope, MC. When I told you I'd never heard of anybody called that, I was speaking the truth. But I'd only to catch sight of him to be pretty certain I'd seen him before, and in some kind of sinister context. Nothing more specific than that till this morning when I woke up remembering who he was and where I'd seen him. I still couldn't remember his original name, and I knew it wasn't him in the flesh I'd seen, just a few photographs, which did nevertheless belong to a sinister context.

'Two. Guy Burgess and Donald Maclean. Do they mean anything to you, Lucy?'

'Not much. Weren't they Communist spies, years ago?'

'Eleven years ago to be precise, in 1951. At any rate, that was when they were exposed and fled to Russia, where they still are.'

'Oh yes, our security coppers made a frightful boob.'

'Not really. It was the weekend and they couldn't get hold of anyone to sign the warrants for the arrests. Respect for the law.'

'Something pretty boobish about that.'

'I agree it could never have happened in Russia.'

'M'm. I accept the rebuke,' said Lucy. 'But how did you know about the warrants?'

'It's not a secret. But the answer to your question takes us to Three. Edward Saxton, D. Litt. Where's this pub I've heard so much about?'

'You can see it from here.'

'So I can. Before we get there, let me just say that about that time I did a bit of work for MI5, to be known henceforth between you and me simply as the company, if you follow me. I'm not in your league as an unfolder of mysteries, but I won't tell you the rest till I've a glass of beer in my hand.'

It was cool, dark and quiet in the saloon bar. Edward and Lucy took their drinks over to a window that gave a view of an unfrequented stretch of road and a green hedgerow with woodland beyond it, all with their colours sharpened by the mild sun. No petrol fumes lingered, only country scents. Edward sipped beer appreciatively.

'One can get tired of drinking wine day in and day out,' he said. 'Though not very soon, I suppose. Now, let me go on briefly. Years ago I helped the company a bit over the matter of defective patriotism among former Cambridge men – you may remember that both Burgess and Maclean had been undergraduates at that university. There were others never or not yet brought to book, half a dozen of them, among whom was the man now known as Colonel Procope, who escaped prosecution for lack of evidence. Nothing could have been proved either against his close friend, perhaps more than close friend, whom I knew as Green, but evidently Green was up to something our side didn't know about, because he cleared off to Russia too, just three weeks after good old Guy and Donald. Green read English at Cambridge, which isn't exactly incompatible with an interest in literature, though I agree—'

'I take it Green is still in Russia. But if he gets the colonel's message he'll soon be on his way back.'

Edward frowned and looked worried. 'I wish we could do better, but I don't think we can at the moment.'

'So what's our next step?'

'I don't honestly see we've got one. What we have is surmise, and nobody seems to be even contemplating anything illegal, I'm sorry to say. It would be interesting to have a tap put on Procope's telephone, but also out of the question. All we can do is keep our eye on the paper.'

'Would it help if we knew how he got them to print that stuff?'

'I'll have a word with the company. About that and other matters.'

Lucy looked at Edward, who held her gaze. She said, 'I'd never have taken you for a . . .'

'Careful.'

'. . . tradesman as well as an expert on Gray.'

'Tradesmen come in all sizes and shapes. What time is lunch?'

As they were on their way out, the landlord nodded politely to Edward and said to Lucy, 'How's my old friend Boris?'

'Oh, he's fine, thank you, Mr Littlejohn.'

'Have you taken him on a proper excursion yet?'

'I thought next week, perhaps.'

'He'd enjoy it,' said the landlord, who with his neat suit and generally scrubbed appearance looked like the citified person he was not. Laying a polished horseshoe on the counter, he said, 'Anyway, here's a present for him.'

'Oh, he'll absolutely love that. I'll nail it on his stable door.'

II

Revision, especially of the Metaphysicals, and bad weather combined to put off the day on which Lucy ceremonially nailed the horseshoe to Boris's stable door. But when that day came it was so clear and bright and the forecast so promising that she planned a proper excursion for him and her on the morrow.

She was up at six and, with her old tweed coat over her nightdress, fetched the horse to his stable facing the kitchen and put chaff and corn in the manger for him. A heavy dew sparkled on the grass, the sky was a slightly veiled but cloudless blue, and there was the kind of hush everywhere that she had noticed before at the start of a fine hot day. She got more or less ready before cooking herself a substantial breakfast of fried egg, bacon and tomatoes, no more than sensible before a day's riding. By this time the paper had arrived and she glanced at it as she ate.

Her eye was caught by a short item saying that the supposed additional stanzas of Gray's *Elegy*, the discovery of which was recently reported, had been shown to be a modern forgery. The finder's request for continued anonymity was being respected. This information revived Lucy's almost-lapsed interest in the matter, and even brought her a mental picture of Colonel Orion Procope being completely indifferent to the news, but she dismissed it and him from her mind in the course of making sandwiches with fresh Cheddar, chopped onion and plenty of sweet pickle. This done, she prepared a thermos of tea, leaving enough tea over to take up to her parents' bedroom with some arrowroot biscuits she privately considered dead boring.

The grandfather clock in the hall struck eight; time for grooming and saddling up. Lucy's saddle, a birthday gift, was of army pattern, which meant among other things that it had plenty of hooks on which to hang a haversack with her provisions, a nosebag with Boris's stuff, her black fisherman's sweater and a blanket of his. She was ready, and of course he knew it at once and made for the outdoors. A minute later she was walking him down towards the road, quite a striking figure in her twill jodhpurs and man's shirt, hair drawn back under a dark-green scarf, with the upright posture Edward had noticed.

As the sunshine grew stronger, the two of them were making good time, mostly over grassland or greenwood floor, so good that Lucy began to think she would fulfil her hope of reaching the coast before turnabout time and showing Boris the sea, perhaps taking him for a gallop along the sands if the tide was right, for a paddle if not. She had been talking on and off to him since they started, and when she mentioned these possibilities he turned his ears back to listen, but on being asked how he felt about them he simply took no further interest.

From earlier outings with Virginia, Lucy was confident that somewhere along their line of march she would find a good place for a rest, and sure enough not long after one o'clock they came to a shady spot with a patch of turf next to the road and a culvert over a stream, only a little one but enough to water Boris and wash the dust off his feet. Then, having loosened his girth, she put on his nosebag and he munched contentedly, swishing his tail against flies. She ate sandwiches, drank half her tea and read a chapter of her paperback copy of *Dr Zhivago*. Before they moved on she got into the saddle and let him crop grass for a few minutes.

Lucy was expecting to come in sight of the sea quite soon when she realised she was heading more or less directly for the village near which Colonel Procope lived. A glance at the map she carried in her haversack showed her that by the shortest route she was about two hours' easy riding-time from it. That route, however, involved a longish stretch of road and, although Boris never complained, she knew he preferred to avoid road travel where possible, so a few minutes later she turned aside on a more roundabout approach. Only then did it occur to her to wonder how long it was since it had first entered her head to seek out the colonel and what she hoped to achieve by doing so. She found no answer to either question, and soon put them aside in favour of taking in the look of sunlit greenery and wild flowers and the lulling pleasure of having a healthy, strong, good-natured horse under her. But she still moved along a curving path that led to Procope's village.

When at length she reached it she found little to see: a few smartened-up cottages, some boring modern houses, a church decorated in the usual flint, but also a post office, and that was obviously her first port of call. With the sound of rock music in her ears, she tied Boris to a convenient rail and went inside among picture post-cards and toffee bars as well as stamps and telegram forms.

Instead of a fat old woman with glasses and a pencil stuck in her hair, Lucy found a fresh-faced one little older than herself, in dark slacks and a tee-shirt bearing the name and device of a brand of American cigarette. No less unexpectedly, this person reduced the music to almost nothing without being asked, and smiled a welcome.

'Colonel Procope?' she said at once when the name was mentioned. 'Straight down the hill over there, lane at the bottom on the left, a bit under a mile along on the left. Say twenty minutes' walk. I suppose it'd be quicker on horseback. That is your horse out there, is it?'

'Thank you. Yes.'

'Work at a riding stable, do you?'

'No. No, he's my very own horse. I keep him at home and look after him there myself.'

'That's nice,' said the young woman vaguely. She looked out of the window and then over her shoulder before glancing at Lucy and away again. 'You, er, excuse me asking, but would you be a great friend of his worship the colonel?'

'Certainly not. My parents see him occasionally but only as a neighbour.'

Lucy thought this description sounded pretty hollow, but it evidently reassured the other girl, who said with another smile, 'I thought you weren't, well, his type, kind of thing. Er, he's not exactly popular round here at the moment.'

'What's he been up to?'

'Not that he's ever been very highly thought of in these parts, but just the other day, see, he went too far. One of the village lads, young Tommy, well, he's only a boy, really, not too bright if you know what I mean, anyway, Tommy was playing round the colonel's place, just like a kid, you know, he wouldn't be doing any harm, and his nibs flies into a tremendous rage, shouts at him, says he'll give him a thrashing if he doesn't make himself scarce that minute. Then laughed and said he was only joking.'

Lucy thought for a minute. 'Did Tommy tell you all this?'

'His mother had to like drag it out of him.'

'Rough luck on poor little Tommy. Did he say anything else?'

'No. Oh, there was one bit, he said there was something funny about the shed in the colonel's garden.'

'M'm. What sort of something funny? I suppose he didn't say.'

'Not really. Something about a hole. His mother said he sounded frightened.'

The girl behind the counter herself spoke with sudden reluctance, as if she repented a little of having been so informative. Lucy took her cue, bought a couple of chocolate biscuits and departed.

Twenty minutes later the biscuits were inside Boris and he was standing in the shade and out of view while Lucy, also out of view, sat looking down on Colonel Procope's domain. This consisted of a small stone-dressed cottage of no particular consequence, a couple of wooden outbuildings and a fragment of land with a spinney at one end and an open gateway on to the road or lane. This was a rough-and-ready affair that on one hand became no more than a track and on the other led to a bridge across a considerable stream. On the far side of the little valley, a more serious road led westward towards Ipswich, Cambridge and other important places.

Nobody was to be seen moving around or near the cottage, not even through the modest but serviceable pair of field glasses that Lucy habitually carried in her haversack and had hitherto shown her nothing more dramatic than the odd pair of nesting waterfowl. It was more than likely that there was nobody in the cottage either. The sense of adventure that had uplifted her since she had reached the village began to subside, leaving her with a half-memory of more childish would-be exploits, adventures of the mind founded on reading and day-dreaming. She was on the point of calling off her fruitless vigil, remounting Boris and making for home – it was too late now for any trip to the coast – when a large dark-blue car she had glimpsed across the valley came into her view again making for the cottage. In due time it slowed up, drove through the gateway, stopped, set down a figure she recognised without her field glasses as the eccentric colonel. Lucy had calculated that one or other of the outbuildings must be a garage, but if so Procope made no immediate use of it; instead, he went and unlocked the door of a small shed. Seen through her glasses now, he looked carefully about him before going inside. Though Lucy had no fear of being seen as long as she kept still, she found this intensive survey disturbing in some way. It took a full half-minute to complete, at the end of which time he did enter the shed and no doubt locked the door after him. There was no sign of the younger man who had acted as chauffeur in the past, nor of anybody else.

Lucy waited without result. She was again about to leave when she saw the door of the shed open and Procope emerge. After locking up once more, he gave a somewhat abbreviated repeat of his all-round scrutiny, then moved to the front of his cottage, which was out of her view, and presumably went in at the front door. When another ten minutes had passed without incident, she left her observation post, went to reassure Boris, who stood placidly tethered to a handy tree, and walked down the grassy slope towards Procope's abode, expecting any moment a challenging shout at best. None came. Still nothing happened when she reached the shed and peered in through a small window.

The interior was dark, and her own reflection kept hampering her attempts to see inside, but quite soon she found a vantage point that gave her a limited view. It was not so limited that she failed to make out part of a shallow trench dug in the earth floor of the shed at one end. So that was the hole young Tommy had seen: a trench. But what was a trench doing in a shed? Was it a trench?

Lucy's heart had begun to beat fast. Trying not to think, only to act, she hurried back to Boris and rode in a sort of semicircle along the slope, down and back till she was approaching along the lane from the village. At Procope's gate she dismounted, having done just enough thinking to run up an elementary story about finding herself in the district with time to spare and paying a call on the off chance that he would be at home.

The front door of the cottage had an old-fashioned bell pull that set up a tuneless jangling somewhere inside. Nothing happened for so long that Lucy had almost made to ring again when the door was flung open to reveal Colonel Procope.

The declining sun clearly illuminated a look of eager welcome on his face which very soon gave place to puzzlement, consternation, anger if not more. 'What do you want?' he demanded. 'What are you doing here?'

She had her back to the light; she was far from his mind; her hair was hidden; he had never done more than glance at her. These points occurred to her later; for the moment she was aware only that he had not recognised her. It seemed to her suddenly important to remain unrecognised. 'I'm sorry, sir,' she said, trying to look as well as sound rustic and gawky, 'but I wondered if my horse could have a drink of water.'

'Certainly not! Get out!' He was shouting and glaring, his fierce eyes doubly strange under the brown thatch of hair. 'If you don't, if you're not gone by the time I finish talking' – his voice rose to something like a scream and a fleck of saliva hit her cheek – 'I promise you I'll set my dogs on you *and I won't be calling them off!*'

There was no need on Lucy's part for any mimicry of someone badly disconcerted and frightened. She was back in the saddle, and had cantered a hundred yards towards the village, before she had time to reflect that any available dogs of the sort implied would assuredly have made a tremendous noise at the first sound of an unexpected visitor. Later still it occurred to her that no horse needed to be taken in search of water with a whole river a bare hundred yards away, but that was not going to matter now.

She arrived back at the post office in time to get some change and was soon on the telephone to Edward's college, to the porter there who advised her to ring the old mill house, then to Edward himself who listened to her account of events without asking any questions, except where he would find her on his arrival in something under the hour. Lucy went to the saloon bar of the designated pub on the far side of the village green, which was nice enough but not as nice as Mr Littlejohn's, and very slowly drank a half-pint of shandy (heavy on the lemonade).

Bit by bit her excitement ebbed away and with it all pretence of certainty, all her former sense of having happened to catch Colonel Procope on the point of committing some fearful atrocity. He had responded with surely disproportionate anger to a stranger's innocent intrusion, for such it had been to his knowledge, and had perhaps shown something of the same earlier to young Tommy. There were a dozen possible explanations for that. He was secretive about his shed, inside which he had dug a trench, and that trench might to a fevered fancy like her own – she admitted it now to herself – have been a grave. And it might have been an unknown number of other things besides. He, the colonel, had fabricated eight lines in the general style of a two-hundred-year-old poem to send a message to a friend who quite likely had been a spy. What had Edward called the basis for that notion? Surmise, perhaps leaving a ruder word unspoken. What he would call her more recent notions Lucy dreaded to think.

Her heart sank further when at last he arrived. She knew immediately from the way he looked round the bar, spotted her, came over, greeted her with a touch of solicitude, that he had not taken her tale seriously. He had turned up for merely avuncular reasons, to give her moral support and to calm her down. His manner was studiedly non-committal when she acted on his request to go over things again.

'So according to you,' said Edward after listening to her, 'you surprised the colonel just as his friend Green, having received and acted on his message, was about to walk in, be killed and be buried in the garden shed. Well now, why would the colonel want to kill his old mate after so elaborately persuading him to come all this way?'

'I don't know,' said Lucy, adding stoutly, 'but that doesn't mean there couldn't be a reason.'

'True, as far as it goes. How, do you think, would the colonel have known so exactly when Green was due after his long and difficult journey? And how might he have induced Green to call on him?'

'He's on the telephone.'

'True again. If Green was indeed going to appear, he might do so at almost any hour of any day out of, let's say a hundred.'

'Yes.'

'But you happened to come along and poke your nose in at the precise time he was expected.'

Lucy said forcefully, 'That's right, perhaps I did, and it's no argument against the manifestation of an unlikely coincidence to notice that such a manifestation, though perfectly possible, is unlikely.'

'True a third time. I think. Now I'm going to have a large glass of whisky. What about you? Would you like something of the sort yourself?'

'No, thank you.' She was slightly astonished. 'What, what for?'

'To strengthen you against a coming ordeal, or what

may very well turn out to be one. We're off back to the colonel's place to see what we can catch him at.'

'Oh, are we? Wouldn't it make more sense to wait till dark?'

'He'll be on his guard then, and I want to see the ground in the light. The sooner we're there the better.'

When Edward had returned from the counter with his whisky, she said, 'Have you told, you know, your friends in the company about any of this?'

He hesitated briefly. 'No.'

'Because you don't want to look ridiculous. As ridiculous as you think my story is.'

Dropping all lightness from his manner, and focusing his attention on her in a way he had never done before, he took her hands in a loose but strong grip. 'I think it only just conceivable that your story has any substance in it at all. And that's how you feel yourself, isn't it? But I'd be a fool if I didn't follow it up. And I'd be worse than a fool if I didn't do something to repay the trust you showed in me when you asked me to help you.'

She was not sure she understood all the meaning behind his words, but she caught his tone immediately and responded to it. 'I'm ready whenever you say.'

He gave a wide grin with his eyes fixed on hers, another new expression, and squeezed her hands for a moment. 'Good. Now where's that horse of yours?'

'I suppose you mean Boris. He's on the green outside here, or he was when I last looked.'

'Yes, I thought I saw him,' he said without much conviction, half got up, remembered his whisky and drained it. 'Right. Order of march. You lead on Boris. I follow in my trusty shooting-brake, which I should like to pull up and put somewhere out of the way a couple of hundred yards short of the objective. Is that possible?'

'We'll pass a bridge over the river on our right. After

that I'll dismount at a point where you should be able to drive off the road.'

He nodded and they left without further ado. Outside they parted in silence, Edward to his car, Lucy to Boris, who showed no resentment at having had to put up with a pretty dull hour, though he was obviously dying to be off somewhere. Before she put her foot in the stirrup she said to him,

'Now this is probably going to be nothing at all, but on the other hand you may find yourself having to do something pretty serious and grown-up, and I'll be relying on you. Are you ready for that?'

He tossed his head in a twisty, sporty way that showed he was ready for anything.

'Okay. Walk march.'

Behind her, she heard Edward start his engine but did not look back. Down the slight hill they went, left into the lane, up to the bridge. The light was still strong, but anyone would have known that evening was not far off. Colonel Procope's cottage came into sight. Soon afterwards, Lucy dismounted as arranged and led Boris to a point in somebody's field where he would not be disturbed and could not be seen from the road. Here she tied him to a fencing post by a rope long enough to let him graze wthout getting tangled, gave him some bread she had been saving and stroked his forehead and down to his nose. She told him to stay quiet and not to worry, because she would be back for him. Her heart was beating fast again, this time from fear, not of the colonel or whatever he might do but of his doing nothing, nothing out of the ordinary, of his turning out to be up to nothing worth all this fuss.

Edward's demeanour, when she joined him in the lane, quite failed to reassure her. His air of serious concentration, his vigilant peering ahead and around, showed her again that he was doing no more than humouring her and was perhaps already rehearsing his indulgent rebuke of her overheated imagination, fondness for sensational fiction and more. So what actually happened when they got to the cottage came as a surprise as well as a shock to them both.

Before Lucy had had time to do more than wonder what Edward had in mind, someone indoors gave a loud scream. It was a different sort of sound from anything she had heard as part of any film or imagined from reading any book; it might have come from a man or a woman or even an animal, and it set up a violent tingling at the back of Lucy's neck, hot or cold, she could not tell which. There were other noises too that might have been bodies striking against furniture. Somewhere at the back a door opened. Edward caught her arm and led her a few yards in that direction before dropping into a crouch behind an evergreen bush and pulling her down beside him. They heard a shout or two, not nearly as loud as the scream, and then a man unknown to them came out through the doorway in an irregular walk, very much like somebody trying to make his way along the deck of a ship in rough weather. He had not gone far when he collapsed on the ground near a water butt, though his arms and legs still moved.

So far, things had seemed to happen slowly, but now they greatly speeded up. Another man, one with blood on his forehead, one recognisable as Colonel Procope, came running out of the cottage and flung himself on top of the man on the ground. It was hard to follow details, but soon a voice said or called something and the first man no longer moved. The colonel got to his feet and stood for a moment, swaying slightly and panting and looking down at the other, who was dead; Lucy had never seen death before, but she found she knew it when she saw it. Then the colonel took the corpse's wrists in a businesslike way and started to drag it face upwards towards the shed.

'That's Green,' Edward muttered to Lucy and at once sprang up and ran towards the two figures. She followed. Procope turned and saw Edward and gave him a blow that sent him down into an all-fours position. Lucy went for the colonel, who hit her on the side of the jaw with his fist. She too went down, afraid she might be sick, able to see but not very well, as if through a flyscreen. By the time she was fully herself again, Colonel Procope had shut the door of his expensive car and was driving off, scattering gravel from under his tyres as he turned into the lane. Edward followed, but some distance behind, and when Lucy reached him he had already given up the chase.

'Damn,' he said. 'He can't get far, but he might—'

'You never know. Come on,' she said, running past him.

He came up with her. 'I'll never catch him in my car.'

'I've got another idea' – one she thought was hopeless but was going to try.

'It's no good.'

'Just run.'

Lucy soon forged ahead. She had won both the 100 yards and the 220 in her last year at school, but she had run no faster then than now, despite her riding clothes. Her speed may even have increased when she saw ahead of her that, in his haste, Colonel Procope had overshot the bridge and was now backing and trying to turn his car. At one point he must have stalled, for she heard the high rattle of the starter. Then she had run far enough, and at her best speed hurried to Boris, unhitched him and got him back to the lane in time to meet a flushed and gasping Edward.

'Get up behind me,' she said from the saddle. She could see the colonel's car crossing the bridge.

'What are you—'

'Do as I say.'

He managed it somehow. Apparently unaffected by the double load, Boris made good time down to the river and stoutly set about carrying them across the ten-yard stream. The water, so cold it burned, reached her knees. That was the end of her remaining sandwiches. Edward's arms were fast round her middle. She heard the approaching sound of the car. Then they were across and Edward swung himself clear and scrambled up the short slope to the edge of the road, putting his hand inside his jacket as he moved. He turned and faced the oncoming car and what happened next seemed to happen all at once. Lucy heard a loud noise between a pop and a sort of sharp crash and again, although she had never heard a revolver fired before, she recognised it. The car swerved away from her, then towards her, narrowly missing her before it ran on to the verge on the river side and stopped there as suddenly as if it had run into a brick wall.

Boris, who had endured the events of the last minute with the calm of a police horse, blew down his nostrils. Edward turned to Lucy and took her hands more tightly than before. His look just then reminded her of the Edward of years before, when he had been a noted cricketer with, she remembered hearing, an aggressive batting style. For no reason she was aware of, tears sprang to her eyes.

'I'm not thinking of him,' she said, not knowing whether she meant Green or Colonel Procope or the two together.

'Neither am I,' said Edward.

Near them, Boris contentedly stamped and snorted.

III

'One bit of news,' said Edward. 'The bullet missed not only him but his car. Some shooting, what? I never could learn even how to hold one of those things.'

'Just as well. But what happened?'

'Well, let's say he spun the wheel round with some idea of spoiling my aim, saw he'd swung too far, went the other way, also too far, and drove straight into a hunk of stone he probably never even saw, fast enough to cause him to bash his head in on the inside of his car. Not a man to react coolly to sudden difficulty or danger, the late colonel. As earlier actions of his had suggested.'

Lucy looked out of the pub window towards the green hedgerow, more brightly sunlit now than when she had last seen it. 'I suppose we'll never know what Green had on him that made him worth the colonel's while to dispose of.'

'In the colonel's own far from infallible estimation. What a silly fellow, as well as a thundering nasty one. Our friends in the, er, our competitors were well advised not to trust him with anything of great importance. No, I think you and I probably wouldn't say thank you for being told the secret of Colonel Procope. What a damn silly name. Can I tempt you to another of those?'

'Thank you, Edward, in a moment.' She went on in bit-by-bit style, 'You know . . . when I telephoned you that evening, and got you to come out and meet me, I realise now it was all fantasy, really. I just wanted to have a lovely storybook adventure, with you in it. Schoolgirl stuff.'

Edward said quickly, before he could think better of doing so, 'I wondered whether it might be something like that, but it didn't bother me at all. I wanted to see you. That was enough.'

'Oh. But you brought your pistol with you.'

'So I did.' He laughed. 'Just company training. Motto, better safe than sorry. Well, your adventure duly turned up, didn't it?'

'It certainly did. That was just as well too.'

'You wouldn't have managed any of it but for Boris. How is the old boy?'

'Oh, he's fine, thank you.' She spoke hurriedly and without warmth.

'What's wrong? Come on, Lucy, is there something the matter with him?'

'No, he's as fit as a fiddle. It's just, I've decided to put him up for sale next week.'

'What?' Edward was genuinely amazed. 'What on earth for?'

'I think I'm getting a bit old to go on having a horse in that adolescent way.'

He nodded slowly. Something her father had said on that point narrowly failed to reach his consciousness. 'Well, I suppose you know best. Are you ready for that drink now?'

'Did anything more ever come out about that forgery?' asked Roger Ashby.

Edward looked up from his armchair and glass of sherry. 'Forgery?'

'Those verses from Gray's *Elegy*, wasn't it? Which you seemed convinced were the work of some forger.'

'Ah. My conviction proved to be well founded. At least it was confirmed by an announcement to that effect in the paper.'

'Really. I must have missed that. Who was the forger, were we told?'

'No. Probably someone quite obscure or even unknown. A mere amateur.' After some hesitation,

Edward went on, 'Oddly enough, just the other day I happened to run across the fellow who brought the verses to light. Bumped into him at a social gathering. He struck me as rather uncommunicative. My impression was he realised he'd been taken for a ride.'

Ashby did not ask for a clarification of the last phrase. 'I'd give something to know how he got a load of tosh into the paper. Friends in high places?'

'Perhaps a kindred spirit. A colleague of mine is looking into it. Now I must leave you for a while. I have to see a man about a horse.'

'A *horse*? That doesn't sound like your kind of thing at all, Edward.'

'Oh, not to lay a bet, I assure you. I'm buying the animal. With a view to giving it back to the vendor as a sort of present.'

'Somebody's birthday?'

'I suppose you could call it an engagement present.'

A Twitch on the Thread

I

'It must be wonderful, never to need help. I simply can't imagine what it's like.'

'I have quite a job myself.' Daniel Davidson tried to match his wife's bantering tone. 'You of all people surely realise I need help constantly, every other waking moment. Every other sleeping moment as well, I expect I'd find if I could be around to check.'

'Oh, come on, you know what I mean – outside help.'

'My kind of help comes from outside too, but yes, darling, of course I know what you mean. How are you feeling this morning?'

This was a regular breakfast-table question that usually got a short non-committal answer. Today it drew another question. 'How do you think I'm looking?'

Daniel surveyed his wife. He saw a pretty, fresh-complexioned woman in her early thirties with thick brown hair, quick eyes and a mouth that had an upward turn. At the moment she seemed to be forcing it to droop at the corners, but without much overall effect. 'You look fine to me,' he said, 'but then . . .'

'But then I always do. My jolly little face, as you once lyrically called it. All bubbling over with the joy of spring. Have you never thought, Daniel, even for a moment, that I might be putting it on, really honestly never? It doesn't matter if you have.'

'Only to start with. Very soon not at all.' He had no

need to ask what it was that she might or might not have been putting on. 'But you still haven't told me how you're feeling.'

'Oh, absolutely terrible, thanks,' said Ruth Davidson comfortably. 'As you've no doubt noticed, I've given up trying to get the voice right. No point in sounding a perfect misery as well as being one. But it's more I wasn't cut out for being one. As if it was happening to the wrong person. I'm sorry, my love.'

'New stuff no good, then?'

'It's a bit early to tell, of course. But I'll stick my neck out and say, well, the clouds might be lifting just a bit. You know there's nothing I'd rather tell you than something more definitely cheerful, but we've been through that and come back again too often.' Ruth took their used tea-mugs across the little basement kitchen to the sink and poured water over them. With her back turned, she said to Daniel, 'The same as there's nothing I'd rather be than just an ordinary woman with a husband she likes a lot and also fancies. I hope you don't need any convincing of that.'

'None whatever, darling,' said Daniel carefully. The care was needed to prevent the least hint of acknowledgement that he had heard very nearly all of this before, and not just in its general drift but down to its finer detail. 'When are you seeing Eric?' He had asked his wife that before, too, with a succession of other names at the end of it.

'We thought today would be about right. It is two weeks since he started me on these new things, but of course I can always hang on till perhaps I know more definitely how I feel.' Ruth checked herself before she could betray how small a hope she had of any profit in hanging on.

'You've made an appointment, have you?'

'Two o'clock. I don't mind cancelling it if you reckon I should.'

Daniel stated firmly that he was sure it would be the right thing to keep the appointment, partly to help Ruth out of taking a sort of decision, but partly because he had taken to Dr Eric Margolis on sight and was starting to believe he might actually do something for her, so presumably the more she saw of him the better. Eric had shown himself to be different from his various predecessors by a businesslike approach that offered no parade of that quality. He claimed merely to have had a good deal of experience and some successes in the treatment of depressive illnesses like the one Ruth appeared to be suffering from. That had sounded good or possibly good to Daniel and still did.

Although it had been nearly six years before, he still remembered often enough and clearly enough the afternoon his wife had come to him in his workroom and, with profuse apologies for interrupting, had confessed that she felt wretched most of the time and often tense and nervous, all without any reason she was aware of. In his experience she seldom wept, but she had wept a good deal while she told him she had hoped never to have to burden him with this and he tried not to give any sign that he had known something like it all along. For once, for a few minutes, he had seen and heard her without – what? Without the face and voice she showed to the world, or rather with a different face and voice, not the real Ruth but another Ruth he dreaded to encounter but had never seen again. Perhaps Eric Margolis had found out how to do so and how to lay to rest that pitiful, driven creature. Meanwhile, he, Daniel, would go on as before, acting as closely and continuously as he could on his wife's appeal not to raise the matter himself in any form.

Reflections of this sort filled the part of his morning that was not taken up with rounding off and revising his article on the ethics of punishment. At noon he gathered his papers and went to take his leave of Ruth. He knew she would tell him if she wanted his company for the Margolis trip and as usual she had evidently decided to manage on her own, so he said only that he would take his piece in to the office and very likely go round to the Sussex for a sandwich with one or two of the lads.

Wearing a red tie to go with his red-and-white check shirt, Daniel smoothed back his long fair hair and left the house, a large healthy-looking man with bright blue eyes that sometimes had a distracted look, hardly believable as the comprehensive-school science-studies teacher he had been before his marriage. The house he left was part of a mid-Victorian terrace that ran dead straight for two hundred yards before reaching the larger street with its coffee shops, little Italian and Greek restaurants, newsagents and video libraries. On the corner opposite the dignified pub stood the hardly less imposing tile-fronted Underground station he was making for.

He had nearly reached it when he caught sight of a middle-aged man standing outside it studying a piece of paper that perhaps bore directions. This and the style of his belted raincoat suggested a foreign visitor of some sort, and Daniel knew he had never seen him before, so it came as a considerable surprise when the man glanced up at his approach and evidently recognised him.

'Hello there, Leo,' said the stranger in an American accent. His expression combined pleasure, astonishment and some less agreeable feeling. 'You're a long way from home, aren't you?'

'What? My name is Daniel Davidson. I'm sorry, you must have mistaken me for somebody else.'

'You're telling me you're not Leo Marzoni? But . . . Talk some more. Please.'

'I don't know what you want me to say. I'm afraid I don't know you.'

'But it's Leo's voice except for the British accent.' By now the man in the raincoat was plainly agitated. 'If you're . . . Mr Davidson, you must have a double. Maybe a twin brother?'

'I have no brother. And no double that I know of. I'm sorry, I can't help you.'

'Sir, would you be good enough to tell me your profession? Your job?'

'Certainly. I'm a clergyman.'

'A clergyman? You mean a priest?'

'A priest of the Church of England, yes.'

'Oh my God,' said the American very quickly. 'Pardon me,' and he hurried away round the corner of the station and was seen no more.

This response to notice of his calling disconcerted Daniel for longer than having been mistaken for Leo something. There were doubtless a number of humdrum possible explanations for that mistake, or apparent mistake, such as researching the British character or winning a bet. Nothing of the sort would account for the unfeigned alarm the man had shown at the end. But Daniel soon forgot the question in the course of travelling from western parts of the capital to somewhere nearer the middle. His reasons for going in by tube included a clear financial one and a confused but strong one to do with what he felt his life should be or include, but on this trip his powerlessness to help his wife was enough to think about.

What with one thing and another, he was more than usually conscious today of being a bloody parson, as in unregenerate or inattentive moments he was still apt to think of himself. At the newspaper building, the features editor greeted him with his usual staunch cordiality, demonstrating to whom it might concern that he, Greg Macdonald, was not the sort to think any the less of a chap merely because he had seen fit to become a rev. Or so Daniel sometimes fancied. The other, smaller man in Macdonald's office had been about to depart, but changed his mind after grasping who and what Daniel must be. While Macdonald read through the article on punishment, this smaller man kept glancing at Daniel in a manner he perhaps believed to be unnoticed. His general air suggested someone thrown by chance into the proximity of an astronaut or serial killer. Daniel had grown used to that kind of reaction, though it seldom took such visible form.

Macdonald finished his reading and nodded weightily for a time. Then he said, still weightily, 'Very good, Dan. Well up to your usual high standard. Thank you.' He went on more buoyantly, 'Just a couple of small points. Mosaic law. They'll think that's something to do with mosaics. Can we call it the law propounded or whatever by Moses?'

'Will they know who Moses was?'

'They'd better. Enough of them will. This is a serious newspaper. Right, if you've no objection. Oh yes. Penology.'

'They'll think that's something to do with pricks,' said the small man, laughing aloud and looking Daniel in the eye.

'Oh Christ, you're still here, are you?' Macdonald twisted round elaborately in his chair. 'Didn't you hear me say the *Sun* ran it one day last week? Well, I did and it did. And there is the telephone if you think of anything more.'

'Nice talking to you,' said Daniel as the small man finally went.

'Number three on the showbiz desk,' said Macdonald.
'Sorry about that. I hate that clever baiting stuff.'
'It's a form of respect really.'
'I suppose you get a lot of it.'
'Not as much as I'd like, or ought to like.'
'You mean it's better than indifference.'
'I suppose that's what I mean,' said Daniel. 'But there are grades of indifference too, you know. I prefer it when it's founded on a fact or two. Now I'm pretty well indifferent to the Pope, let's say, but I'm clear about who he is.'

'I don't know a hell of a lot of fellows like you, Dan, but you're the only one I do know that doesn't mind talking about religion. And yet, it's funny, you look to me more like a cricketer or a racing-driver than . . .'

'Than a bloody parson. I know you mean that kindly. Will the study of methods of punishment do you instead of penology?'

When they got to the Sussex, they found already there the elderly urchin who was the assistant editor and the distinguished-looking scholarly type who was the astrologer, the latter said to be the chief agent of the paper's healthy and still rising sales. Their greeting to Daniel was heartier than Macdonald's had been but also more uneasy, as if he had just come off none too well after a charge of kerb-crawling. But they were tremendously unselfconscious about asking for whisky in his presence, and did not even glance at his ginger beer when it came, let alone at each other. Daniel sympathized with their embarrassment, which he saw as no reflection on them, and respected their efforts to hide it. Very soon it would all have worn off, and he had almost stopped noticing it in them at any stage, and about time too.

He and Macdonald carried their sandwiches over to a small table by the wall. After a couple of minutes Macdonald said,

73

'You read the latest piece from that chap the Bishop of Kesteven, sounding off again?'

'Yes, thanks. Do you want me to write something about it or him? I wouldn't be the only one.'

'That doesn't matter to us. I thought it might come in nicely for your next. The importance of individual responsibility. Made to measure for you, Dan.'

'It might be fun to have a crack at it. And him.'

'What's he like? Do you know him?'

'A bit, yes. "Call me Barry" Kesteven is a pleasant, talkative fellow a few years older than me, say early forties. He'd make a useful video-shop proprietor, the sort that puts aside stuff he thinks you'll like. Not at all what you might expect from a servant of the Devil.'

Macdonald grinned a little fixedly. 'Do you mean all that seriously?'

'What, that the Devil exists, et cetera? You bet I do, mate, and I'd advise you to take the same line yourself if you know what's good for you. All right, I'll do Barry. You'd better send me a xerox, if you would, of what he actually said or wrote. Can I get you a drink?'

Daniel went and came back with another ginger beer for himself and another whisky for Macdonald, who asked, 'How long is it now?'

'Oh, it must be . . . Sorry, it's some time since I worked it out. Well, it'll be eight years this coming 10th August. No, actually that was the day I took my last drink, so it has to be the 11th I started on the ginger beer.'

'Was that before or after you met Ruth?'

'I'd just got through my second week off it when she turned up. That was the way round things were in those days.'

There was no trace of staunch cordiality in Macdonald's voice or manner when he asked, 'How is she these days?'

'Much as usual, but there are signs she's starting to get a little more cheerful.' Daniel always said something along those lines anyway when people asked something like that, merely to avoid spreading gloom.

'Good,' said Macdonald when nothing more seemed to be on offer. 'I hope I didn't . . .'

'Absolutely not. It's just that no news is no news.'

When Daniel got back home he thought several times of telephoning Eric Margolis to make quite sure that as regards Ruth's state of mind there was indeed no news, but each time he decided against it. The Davidsons' bottom two floors of the house were empty. They had lived there since a few weeks after their marriage, and for some time after that he had wondered occasionally how a baby might have been fitted in there, but he never wondered about that now. He made himself a pot of tea and waited for Ruth to come back. When sufficient time had passed, he decided she must have gone on to see someone, perhaps her sister in Westbourne Park. The couple who lived on the upper floors were both out at work, and the only sounds he could hear came from outside the building. When he had finished his tea, he went up to the ground floor and into his workroom above the kitchen. There, in a spot beside the desk from which he could see the trees at the end and along the side of the small garden, he knelt and prayed as he did a couple of times every day. After thanking God for his mercies, he petitioned as always for removal or alleviation of Ruth's sufferings by any fitting means, spiritual or physical or a blend of the two. Then, with a few reminders from his notebook, he appealed for the various forms of divine help needed by some of his parishioners. Finally he went through his list of late afternoon and evening visits, telephoning to check one or two doubtful cases.

Before he went out to start his round, Daniel rang Eric after all and was told Ruth had seemed to show no spectacular improvement if indeed any had been measurable. But, said Eric with ferociously guarded optimism, the possibility of some turn for the better some time in the future should certainly not be ruled out.

II

Over the next few weeks nothing changed much. Ruth's state continued to give grounds for modest hope that it might one day mend. Daniel's article on the utterances of the Bishop of Kesteven drew some correspondence in the newspaper and an approving reference in the *Spectator*. Daniel himself officiated at two weddings and several cremations, gave a communion service on the Thursday mornings, read the *Church Times* every Friday, attended the monthly meeting of the Parochial Church Council, prepared and delivered a weekly sermon.

One Saturday morning he was typing out such a sermon when Ruth came into his workroom and said, 'There's a man watching the house.'

He got to his feet. 'Sit down and tell me about it, darling.'

'I haven't started going mad,' she assured him cheerfully, 'if that's what you're thinking. There just *is* a man watching the house. Most interesting.'

'What sort of man?'

'The funny thing is, I haven't been able to see his face, he's got sunglasses on for one thing, but I've got the feeling I know him. You see what you think.' On the way to their bedroom, which was on the same floor at the front, she said, 'I suppose he might be waiting for somebody or have decided he could do with a bit of a

76

read, but to me he looks like a man watching the house. I don't know, perhaps having mistaken it for another house. There, see?'

What Daniel saw without difficulty was a man of about his own size and shape, wearing sunglasses as noticed and holding a newspaper that hid another part of his face. After a short inspection it became hard to believe he was actually reading his newspaper and quite easy to agree with Ruth about what he was up to.

'How long ago did you spot him?' Daniel asked her.

'It must be getting on for ten minutes now. He hasn't moved since.'

'I don't think í know him.'

At that point, the man on the pavement tucked his paper under his arm and took off his glasses and wiped them. Daniel moved to get a better view, perhaps over-abruptly or unduly fast; anyway, just then the man looked up and at last showed his face, or enough of it to be recognizable by somebody with good eyesight at that sort of range. This Daniel had. He also had strong nerves, which helped him not to respond to what he had seen in a way many might have, with a cry of surprise or alarm. As it was he gave a violent start and drew in his breath sharply.

Ruth caught him by the arm. 'What's the matter?'

'Oh God, didn't you see? Surely . . .'

'Daniel, what is it?'

'You didn't see.' With great reluctance he looked again where he had been looking before, and saw no one. 'The . . . fellow seems to have gone now.'

'Who was he? Did you know him? Please tell me.'

'In a minute. Let's go back next door first.'

In his workroom once more, he made straight for his desk-chair and sat, thinking to himself that if there had been drink in the house he might very well have made straight for that instead. Ruth took the only other chair in the room. When he was breathing normally again, he said,

'I'm sorry, my love, I didn't mean to frighten you, but I had a bit of a scare myself. Just for a second I could have sworn that the chap outside was me, or the dead spit of me, or very nearly, to an uncanny degree. Quite a shock in a way. Of course I realise now he was just very like me. Nothing terribly odd about that. My face is the sort of face a lot of chaps have.'

'I don't think so,' said Ruth, 'but then I'm biased. Anyway, I've got it now, he wasn't just very like you, he was the absolute image of you, he was your double. You were right the first time: he was you.'

'I thought you didn't see his face.'

'I didn't have to. I could tell by the rest of him and the way he was standing. I almost got it the moment I saw him the second time because I'd seen you in between. You thought he was only, how did you put it, very nearly the image of you because all the millions of times you'd seen his face before it was the wrong way round. In your mirror.'

'Maybe,' said Daniel. 'Well, plenty of people have doubles. But . . .' He paused abruptly.

'But why should one of them come and spy on the other?'

Before Daniel could have spoken, the front-door bell rang.

'Don't answer it,' said Ruth.

'It's all right, darling, I promise you.'

Daniel went and opened the door. His double stood on the step, fair hair worn a little shorter than his own but still left long and parted in the same place, bright blue eyes, generally healthy looks, perhaps half an inch shorter, dressed differently but not so differently.

'You must be the Reverend Daniel Davidson.' The accent was American.

'I am he. And you must be Mr Leo Marzoni.'

'Correct. But I'm not only that, I'm your twin brother. Did you know I existed?'

'No.'

'Nevertheless I do, as you see, and that is what I am. But I have the advantage of you: I knew about you already. If you like to ask me in I can tell you more.'

'Please come in,' said Daniel mechanically. 'I'm sorry, I wasn't thinking.'

'Oh, you're forgiven,' said his visitor, with a sudden smile that communicated no warmth. 'The circumstances are out of the ordinary.'

Ever since he heard the bell ring, Daniel had been under the delusion that his words and actions were proceeding of themselves, without any need of his premeditation or will. He felt powerless to behave otherwise as he moved back to allow the man called Leo Marzoni to cross the theshold, and did no more than note his own instinct or whatever it was that told him that the other could not be what he said or seemed and that his coming here meant some incalculable harm. These feelings showed no signs of lessening while he took the stranger into his workroom and introduced a startled but not obviously frightened Ruth. Daniel found himself pronouncing words of reassurance to her and others meant to be explanatory about twins and doubles, and went on to tell her something of the American he had run into some weeks previously. Marzoni, on the other hand, appeared to find the situation little more than exceptional, striking, perhaps difficult. In a straight-forward style he apologised for his various antics, for having had the absurd idea of waiting to catch Daniel as he came out of the house and especially for having panicked just now and taken off down the street before having the sense to turn back. He added that he would tell his story in full when they had all had a little time.

By the end of this recital, Daniel had begun to struggle free of his impression that events were taking place somewhere that, despite obvious resemblances, was not the world he knew. But he only really came to himself when the three of them were sitting in the kitchen over cups of coffee and the man he must learn to think of as his brother had duly begun the first instalment of his story. Several instalments were to follow; later, he was able to fit them together in his mind.

Leopold Marzoni was now thirty-eight years old. He had been brought up by a couple whom he treated in every way as his parents and whom he loved as a son, but he could not remember a time when he had not known that he was not biologically their son. He understood from them that he had been born in Brighton, England, and taken to America in infancy. His true mother had died soon after giving birth to him and to his twin brother. Leopold's foster parents had purposely avoided making the least move towards locating or even inquiring after this brother, whom they assumed to have also been adopted but no doubt reared in England. They had felt it their duty to tell Leopold this much, but had also impressed upon him that any attempt on his part to find his twin would be a dubious and almost certainly useless undertaking. Although he could remember, in his childhood, treating a British brother as an invisible companion in times of solitude, he had hardly given the real person a thought for thirty years.

So far, indeed, had that person been from Leopold's mind that he had said nothing of any twin brother when a neighbour, Irving Rothberg, had announced a forthcoming trip to England. But when Rothberg had come to see him on his first day back home and had spoken excitedly of having seen and talked briefly to an Englishman who was Leopold's replica, the latter had given his twin more than a thought. At once he had acted counter to parental advice and set about finding the Englishman in question.

'How did you manage to do that?' asked Daniel.

'It was easy, given Irving's memory. He remembered your name and the fact that you were an Anglican minister, so I got on to your General Synod and they delivered right away. It seems there's a Daniel Davies in Liverpool, but I ruled him out. Too old, for one thing. You must have had quite a shock, Daniel, when Irving sprang into your path and started calling you Leo.'

'I suppose it might have helped if I'd known I had a twin brother.'

'But your foster parents didn't tell you.'

'I didn't have foster parents in your sense, Leo. I was brought up in an orphanage, by an orphanage.' Without either of them being more than half aware of it, Daniel and Ruth joined hands as he said these words. 'They couldn't have been kinder or nicer to me or have done more for me than they did, but no, they didn't tell me I had a brother.'

'I see.' Leopold Marzoni looked almost grim, or at least as though he was coming to a less straightforward part of his tale. 'Not merely a brother, but a twin brother, as you said. And not merely a twin brother, but an identical twin brother, such that you and I look exactly alike. And I mean exactly alike, more alike even than most other identical twins. The nail on your left middle finger is smaller than usual, like mine. Your left eyebrow takes a little turn upward at the end and so does mine. And do you by any chance have a mole shaped like a horseshoe just below your navel? So do I.'

'And the pair of you don't merely look alike, you sound alike,' said Ruth. 'You have the same voice. One moment it talks with an American accent and the next it turns British, but it's the same voice, from the, I don't know, from the same part of the mouth, with the same little hesitations.'

'So Irving noticed,' said Leo, still rather sombrely. 'But you and I, Daniel, we don't merely look alike and sound alike. To understand the extent of our likeness, you need to know something about twins in general, okay? It's pretty solid stuff, so you'd better be sure you want it. No objections? Good, very good. For ease of digestion I'll give it to you in bits. Here comes Part I.'

Most cultures (said Leo) had greeted the occurrence of twins with hostility and even dread. Comparatively recently, attitudes had improved and serious study been possible. This had defined the difference between identical twins, who were always of the same sex, and the much commoner fraternal twins, who were often of unlike sex and no more similar than ordinary brothers and sisters. The difference was primordial and intrinsic.

Monozygotic or MZ twins, popularly known as identical twins, were the separate fruits of a single fertilised ovum that for some reason still under study had split into two. The name emphasised the fact that such twins have identical genes, are clones of each other. Fraternal twins were the product of two discrete fertilised ova and had only half their genes in common. Psychologists, biologists, geneticists and others interested in heredity had studied twins for many years. More lately, research had focused on MZ twins who had been separated soon after birth and reared apart. These individuals were rare, but there were probably a few thousand of them in the contemporary Western world, and recent investigations at Minnesota

University had tracked down and studied more than a hundred of them.

Such was the gist of Part I. Daniel respected his twin's seriousness of purpose, while far from clear what that purpose was. At any rate, by the time Part II began he was seeing Leo as just a man and not as some kind of unearthly visitant.

When such twins were subjected to a full comparison (Leo continued), the close similarities between members of a pair in physical attributes, such as height, fingerprints and hair colour, might have been predicted. What was rather more surprising was the similarity of non-physical attributes such as tolerance, self-control and sociability. But most people would have been very much surprised by something more than similarity in the case of what might be called biographical detail. For instance, such correspondences between a pair of twins as recorded in 1979 included the following, selected from more than thirty such:

('I've been over this so many times I have it off by heart.')

Both men, aged thirty-nine when studied, had married a woman called Linda, divorced her and subsequently married one called Betty.

One twin had named his first son James Alan, and the other had named his James Allan.

Both had been employed by McDonalds and as a filling-station attendant.

Both had white benches built round the trunk of a tree in the garden.

'I'm particularly fond of that last one,' said Leo. 'I have fun imagining some guy who likes to think we're shaped by our environment rather than by our heredity explaining that either as a coincidence in itself or as the result of coincidental similarity in upbringing. Like the paddling in what comes next.'

From twenty-five resemblances in a study of a pair of female twins:

Both had fallen off a fence in childhood and bore scars in the same place.

One had a reasonless chronic pain in the right thigh, the other had a wasted muscle in the right hip but suffered no pain.

They folded their clothes in the same way, and when putting blouses and shirts in drawers, both did up every other button.

Both had developed the habit of walking backwards into the sea when going paddling.

'And just in the event that's not enough to convince you of something,' said Leo finally, 'and before we go any further, my wife, whom I married seven years ago, is called Ruth.'

'Does she look like me?' asked Ruth Davidson.

With only a brief hesitation, Leo said, 'My Ruth is roughly of the same physical type as yourself, fair-complexioned, vivacious in appearance if that's physical. But here, you can see for yourself,' and he took a photograph out of his wallet and laid it on the table between them.

Ruth picked it up, studied it briefly and passed it to Daniel, who saw a pretty woman of about thirty looking rather like his wife, about as much like her as a sister of hers of similar age might have done, perhaps a fraternal twin. He got up and opened the French door into the garden. In fine weather like this the small kitchen could begin to get quite stuffy in the middle of the day. He filled a glass with tap water but set it down after only one sip.

'What sort of temperament would you say your wife has?' he asked Leo.

'As to temperament, well, what shall I say, not as vivacious as her appearance.'

'Depressive?'

'Well, Daniel, I think depressive just like that might be going a little far, you know? But in the right direction. Let's say anxious, nervous, ah, apprehensive? Inclined to fear the worst, is that enough?'

'Yes,' said Ruth, avoiding her husband's eye.

After a silence, Leo went on, 'But I didn't come all this way just to compare notes with you, Dan. It's been wonderful and extraordinary finding you like this, but there's more than that at stake. First, though, do you want us to go to Minnesota and have ourselves examined by scientists? I have to say they'd pay our expenses if we did.'

'No, let's keep this to ourselves.'

'My thoughts exactly. Now, you no doubt recall that when you told Irving Rothberg that by profession you were a minister of religion, he became agitated, because my—'

'You're a clergyman too.'

'Correct, Daniel, and not only that, but a minister of the Episcopal Church, which is the name for the Anglican communion in the States, which makes me as close a replica of you as I could possibly be in that rather important department.'

'Which must have struck your friend Rothberg as a coincidence so far-fetched as to be uncanny,' said Ruth, looking at Daniel now.

'So that was how you knew about the General Synod and the rest of it,' he said.

'Correct again. Now . . . brother . . . do you want to go on a little further, or do you want to stop? For now, that is. Maybe you'd like to stop.'

Looking into the bright blue eyes that were so like his own as seen for dozens of years in mirrors, even looking into them quite briefly, made Daniel feel almost dizzy, if not terrified, then in more serious danger than he had ever thought of in his life before. But as soon as he could he said, trying to sound like a man filling in a form, 'I'd like to go on a little further, such as, when were you ordained, Leo? Of course you know the exact date.'

'Of course. It was March 22nd, 1985.'

'I was 4th April in the same year.'

'Not the same day, at least,' said Leo. He put out his hand in an odd gesture, as if he wanted to give comfort or reassurance, hesitated and drew back.

'Close enough. Nine, thirteen days. And one more thing, if you will. Was your ordination the result of a sudden decision or did you approach it gradually, through stages of belief and conviction and . . .'

'It was sudden. Do you want me to tell you about it?'

'No. No, not now. We've come a long way in a short time. I'd like to have a chance to adjust.'

'I hoped you were going to say that. In fact it wouldn't be overstating the case to say I knew you were going to say that.'

'Oh, I knew it too,' said Ruth. 'That or something to the same effect. Easy enough to see it in his face, sorry, darling, your face, just before you spoke. Anybody could have seen it who happened to be watching you attentively.'

'Which you were certainly doing,' said Leo with a smile.

'Yes, I've been watching you both attentively most of the time we've been down here. And comparing how you look. Now there was a pair of identical twins at my school, at least they said they were identical and they should have known, but they didn't *look* identical much. They were dressed the same sometimes, but nobody ever had any trouble telling them apart. Well, one of them even wore glasses most of the time and the other didn't seem to need them. And one was fatter than the other. Identical – no, what's needed is a word meaning rather more alike than similar. That's what you two are to look at, all you are. Dozens of differences, mostly small, shape of lower lip, left ear, really both ears, where the nose starts – dozens of them. You'd only look *very much* alike at a distance, which is how you first saw each other. There.'

'I never realised you were as observant as that,' said Daniel.

'But what's it all in aid of, you mean. Just, you don't want the two of you to be too much alike, do you?'

Leo nodded vigorously. 'Right, Ruth, right.'

'It's true,' said Daniel. 'I want to be told we're not.'

'Here's another way we're not,' said Leo. 'I'd be – let's say I wouldn't give a damn if we were utterly alike in every way there is.'

'That would make us completely unlike in the most important way of all.'

'Like you said, old buddy, we need to have time to adjust. How are the two of you fixed for later? Can I take you out to dinner?'

'Thank you, Leo, but speaking for myself I don't think I'd feel comfortable. Too much risk of you and me being stared at. You come here.'

Leo grinned. 'I see I mustn't forget that as well as being my twin brother you're an Englishman.'

'True enough. I was thinking we'd find it easier to talk with just the three of us.'

'Well, it's your town. Which I mean to go out and take a look at meanwhile. It's the first time I've ever been in it.'

They made their arrangements and Leo soon went off to the small hotel quite close by where he was staying, setting off on foot as a way of starting his look at London.

'He's got your walk,' said Ruth. 'Or you've got his.' She seemed charged up by recent events, her curiosity and alertness whetted.

'I suppose that's only to be expected.'

'Is that all you can say? Why don't you care for the idea of Leo and you being so alike? Does it give you a sort of weird feeling, doppelgänger stuff, anything on those lines?'

'Nothing like that at all. Plenty of things bother me, as you know, but I'm all right there.'

'I noticed you held back when he went to hug you just now.'

'Me being an Englishman again.'

Ruth frowned and moved her head to and fro at this. A minute later she said, 'Admittedly I haven't had much experience of husbands of mine meeting twin brothers they didn't know they had, but I'd have expected you to be full of questions and excitement and *wonder*, not the way you are now, as if you'd just had a packet of bad news.'

'I'm sorry, Ruth, I'd like to be like you about it, believe me, but bad news is exactly what I'm afraid I've had, or may be going to get.'

'You mean to do with JC?'

'Yes, that's what I – yes, yes.'

'But you can't tell me what or how.'

'I don't know myself, any more than I understand about him and me.' A tear started to run down Daniel's cheek and he wiped it away with his fingers. 'Sorry. If I did I'd tell you about it straight away, you know that.'

'Isn't there anything you can tell me?' she asked gravely.

'Probably nothing you haven't already seen for yourself, but anyway, one question I didn't ask Leo, in fact I expect you noticed me dashing in to stop him answering it before I had time to ask it . . .'

'. . . was if he was a godless drunk one minute and a very serious parson the next.'

Daniel hesitated. Then he said, 'All right, that'll do for the moment. At least if any of it wasn't or isn't true then I needn't worry about the rest. Now I suppose I'd better finish off my sermon for tomorrow. I'll be in for lunch but late. I've got to go and see Miss Rawlings first.'

'Is that the one with the killing eyes and the fantastic figure?'

'No, it's the one with the Edwardian false teeth and the face of a thousand wrinkles.'

He was on his way to the kitchen stairs when Ruth said, 'I wonder why he didn't bring his wife with him. Why he left the other Ruth at home.'

'Economy, I expect. If they're anything like us they have to watch the pennies the whole time.'

'Well, at any rate he's not unlike you. I wonder if they've got any kids.'

'We'll ask him.' Daniel retraced a couple of his steps. 'Doesn't it bother you, being like the other Ruth in temperament as well as looks and even having the same name?'

'Not a bit. You and he would almost certainly be drawn to the same kind of woman, and the name is nothing. Coincidence. Never make the mistake of underestimating the likelihood of coincidence.'

Daniel finished typing his sermon and went over the script pointing it like the text of a psalm and underlining words to be stressed. When he was satisfied, he put on his dicky and dog-collar, picked up his communion case and went out to his car, an A-registered Cavalier parked at the kerb. His parishioners had bought it for him and met some of its bills. Ten minutes later he was pulling up outside an unprepossessing but not actually awful block of flats. Since it was in quite a good area, not on any football supporters' track, for example, he left the car where it was, taking the communion case with him. Miss Rawlings had not so far asked for the service but he hoped she might one day, as some in her circumstances already had.

Miss Rawlings lived on the first floor, across a tidy, well-swept hall and up a stairway that Daniel had sometimes thought would have been the better for a couple of graffiti or some other defilement as a distraction from the overall style of the fittings. There was, however, enough of an unwanted smell coming from her room to offset this deficiency, strange and no more than disagreeable rather than straightforwardly revolting. As he made his way in, Daniel recited to himself supposed facts about the swift overloading of the olfactory sense in man.

Beside Miss Rawlings, sitting next to her on the couch of obsolete plastic, was a woman he knew quite well to be her widowed niece, but who looked at him with uncertainty and misgiving, in her fifties but at sea in the presence of a bloody parson.

'I'll be going then, Della,' she said reluctantly, her eyes on him. 'I thought I'd only just got here, but you seem to have company, don't you? Is there anything you want? I said is there anything you want?'

'Haven't you got that list I gave you?'

'What? Of course I have. I was just wondering if there was anything else. You know, anything else you wanted. You know.'

There was evidently nothing else, nothing on the tip of anyone's tongue at least. Looking successively at the other two as if of course it was no business of hers but she did hope they knew what they were doing, the niece left. Then, asked how she had been over the past week, Miss Rawlings began a narrative that worked up now and then to the level of mild complaint. Daniel had been ready for that. His unspoken agreement with the old lady was that she got a few things off her chest to start with and about the halfway mark it was his turn to talk about God, or at least to approach that subject. He listened now to what she was saying about the language of the girl at the paper-shop, superstitiously hoping that to do so might be repaid by her listening to him for as long.

Eventually Miss Rawlings said, 'My real trouble is I get these nasty times when I don't seem to see the point of somebody like me keeping going at all. I suppose you're going to say that's wrong, Mr Davidson.'

'A lot of people in your sort of situation do feel that from time to time.'

'That doesn't make it wrong or right, does it?'

'Let's just say it's unnecessary.'

'I don't remember ever thinking something because it was necessary. What was it – my sort of situation, you said? You don't know what it's like, how could you?'

Daniel saw that Miss Rawlings's eyes were bright over her fallen-in cheeks and the sharp nose that old age had made prominent. 'No, I don't,' he answered her, 'but now I come to think of it there are plenty of people not in your situation who can't see any reason for carrying on. I used to be one of them myself. Does that surprise you?'

'It's not the same thing at all, a young man like you.'

'Years don't matter, we can desperately need help at any time of our lives, and mercifully help is always available to those who ask for it.'

'I tell you, vicar, there's nobody who's going to help me. My niece and my grandnephew, and Ernie, oh he's marvellous, that Ernie, but what can he do, what can any of them do, they've got their own lives to lead. I need a person with me every minute of the day and night, and how could I expect anybody to put themselves in that position, if they had the time they wouldn't have the patience, how could they? No, I'm sorry, Mr Davidson, you're very good, but I just can't see any point in me going on.'

'You're forgetting God,' said Daniel. 'He'll be with you as long as you want him, he's got the time and the patience for everybody. You only have to ask him.'

'Oh, God,' said Miss Rawlings, by way of amused or weary reference, not invocation, 'don't talk to me about God. I tell you, he's never done nothing for me.'

'Have you asked him, have you prayed to him? It's the same thing, you know. And he always answers, did you know that? I was in such despair once I was going to kill myself, and at the last minute and as a last resort I prayed to God although I didn't believe in him then, but he answered just the same. I found I could . . .'

Daniel let his voice trail off. He had thought or hoped that the importance to everybody of what he was saying was so great and obvious that it was bound to reach someone who at any rate was used to hearing God mentioned. But it seemed that the bright eyes had sunk back into their sockets and the liveliness of manner gone again. A moment ago, the one room had looked neat and even cheerful, the single bed made and spread with a light green counterpane, the sink and draining board clear, with the clean crockery on its rack, a pair of flourishing potted plants on the sill. Now, he saw it as static and lifeless, like a model cell in an enlightened gaol. Poor Miss Rawlings. Even if he had had the required energy and insensitivity, he would still have not dared to tell her any more of the story of his first prayer, not just that it had been answered because he had truly wanted help, but what he had suspected more and more strongly ever since that moment, that God had planted in him the impulse to pray. Faith was offered before it could be accepted. He brought out his pocket diary and turned over some of its pages while he briefly made petition that Miss Rawlings should receive the gift of faith.

'Going, are you, doctor, I mean vicar?'

'Not just yet. There's still time for me to give you a hand with the forms for your new pension-book, that's if you'd like me to.'

'There's just a couple of places I'm not sure about. My niece looked it over, but you know, Mr Davidson, she's really a very ignorant woman, my niece. She's good about clearing the place up, I'll give her that . . .'

From the moment when Leo arrived at the Davidsons' that evening, Daniel felt certain that some disaster impended. Leo was perhaps conscious of a similar discomfort, not showing the buoyant disposition of that morning, when he had seemed to be at worst perfectly resigned to each successive shock of revelation. Daniel was at once drawn to him as one who must be uniquely sympathetic, and repelled by dread of one who constituted a threat to indispensable convictions. Was that normal, reasonable, to be expected in a man confronted with another who was limitlessly the same? Or was the whole concern no more than most singular and interesting? Nothing on paper or anywhere else gave guidance.

Not quite understanding why he did so, Daniel had spent the afternoon getting everything squared away in good time. After seeing to it that the church was ready for early service in the morning, he came back home and made a couple of telephone calls to fix the time of a cremation and brought his diary up to date. Then, as he did every fortnight or so, he wrote to his bishop, a prelate with outmoded ideas about his special responsibilities to those he had ordained. By a self-established tradition, Daniel devoted his final paragraph to a report on how

God had seemed to him over the last weeks and how he thought he might have seemed to God. With feelings of guilt that no inner reasoning would dispel, he confined himself here to what he more or less certainly knew, omitting formless and very likely superstitious presentiments. When the letter had been made ready for the post, he straightened his parishioners file and tidied his workroom. He left as they were the photographs along his mantelpiece except for one showing the woman at the orphanage who, as he supposed, had been like a mother to him. She had been dead for nearly twenty years and the likeness was imperfect, but it was good enough to recall her to him when, as now, he picked it up and studied it. Lastly he knelt and prayed to be forgiven for having done so little to help Miss Rawlings and himself to be helped to face – what? Whatever might be in store.

While Leo and he were settling themselves in the kitchen as before, Daniel started to explain that Ruth would come down in a few minutes when she was ready, but Leo finished his sentence for him. Daniel shifted uneasily in his chair.

'Ah, come on, Daniel, there's nothing in that,' Leo went on. 'Only cause for worry if I couldn't see that coming. You and I could set up a great telepathy act, though. Do these identical twins have identical minds? Or maybe they have only one mind between them. We'd clean up. Too bad God wouldn't like it.'

'You don't believe in any of that paranormal stuff, do you?'

'Of course not, what do you think I am? That's one of the places God comes in very conveniently, isn't it? One word from him and there's no need to bother with that type of dreck for the rest of your life.'

Leo had spoken lightly, in keeping with his words and with his generously cut light-blue suit, darker-blue shirt and rather flashy sea-green tie. He looked altogether unlike Daniel's idea of a parson, even an American one. In fact he looked more like a successful insurance agent or travelling salesman than any member of the professional classes; Daniel recognised, or admitted to himself, that he must have something in his own general appearance that corresponded. Despite these things, however, Leo retained the air of uneasiness detectable as soon as he stepped in from the street. The smile accompanying his last remark seemed particularly forced. Before it had quite faded, he said,

'There was just one thing I wanted to tell you out of your Ruth's hearing, so here goes, why I didn't bring my Ruth to England with me, I thought perhaps you wondered about that.'

'Ruth did, my Ruth did.'

'Yes, she would, I see she would. Maybe I should have told you then, before, but the reason my Ruth isn't here is that she's with another guy. Been with him just two years now. You don't want to hear whose fault it was, even if I knew, it was like this other guy came along and sailed in and collected her. She liked me, but she liked him better. I didn't enjoy the next year at all, but I got through it without falling by the wayside and I'm over it now.'

Nevertheless Daniel said, 'I'm sorry, Leo.'

'Sure you are. I wouldn't have brought it up, but I felt you should know it. I didn't want you wondering, and when I thought about it, well, you needed to hear about something where we aren't the same, and right there is one sizeable thing. And don't forget the guy came along and he collected her, I'll swear she wasn't on the lookout for him or anybody, she wasn't driven out by her depression or anything else, so if you wanted to think my Ruth's departure says something about the likelihood of your Ruth departing you'd have to believe in Santa Claus. Or telepathy. Okay, the name's the same. Coincidence, my friend. Unless you have somebody called Janet in your life? No, I thought not. No more of this, then. I hope I didn't waste your time, Daniel.'

Now Daniel embraced his twin without hesitation and held on. He wondered that he had ever found it more than unfamiliar to be looking at and talking to a man so like himself in appearance. Leo had indeed followed or read his thoughts with remarkable accuracy, perhaps less remarkable in one so like himself on the inside as well. Of course. At this point Daniel pulled himself up as he remembered that Leo had just been talking of an irreparable loss. 'Would you like a drink?' he asked without further thought.

'Thank you, Daniel. If you mean a drink like coffee or lemonade, then not just now; if you mean like gin all the way through beer with any alcohol in it, then still no. But you have some of that kind of drink right here, do you?'

'No, there's nothing. I spoke without thinking. Neither Ruth nor I ever go near real drink.'

'Oh,' said Leo. He looked round the kitchen, seeming to notice the dresser with its rows of plates, the TV set and small low-built radio, the white-painted staircase leading up to the ground floor, the door to the dining-room, the open garden door past which came herbal scents and the distant cries of children. Louder and more sharply than before, he said, 'Did you never touch alcohol? I mean you yourself?'

'Oh, I touched it all right. Not to say bashed it. For years. Then I gave it up altogether.'

'Would you have called yourself a drunk in those days?'

'Yes. At least I agree that's what I was then. I should imagine plenty of people called me it at the time.'

Leo nodded his head, looked at Daniel for a moment and dropped his gaze. 'I don't quite know how to say this, but back then, did you believe in God?'

'No.'

'And . . . did your belief, was your coming to believe connected with your ceasing to be a drunk?'

'Yes,' said Daniel, looking back at Leo. 'It was all part of the same thing.'

'Daniel!' called Ruth's voice from the floor above. 'Darling, could you come up here a minute?'

Ruth was standing in the bedroom in an unfamiliar attitude, elbows crooked and right hand clasping left. She was smiling, with a look of settled anticipation, as if she had been watching him opening a parcel that contained a birthday present she knew he really wanted. She wore a freshly laundered white dress with a pattern of small blue flowers, one he had always liked her in but had not known her to wear for a long time.

'I was going to get you to guess,' she said, 'but then I thought that would be a bit silly, so I'll just tell you. You remember a couple of weeks ago I was boring you about some new stuff Eric had put me on, and I said it was early days yet but I thought there might be a slight improvement? – actually it was more than slight, but I was touching wood, and I've hung on all this time to try and be on the safe side, but anyway, still touching wood, I'm *much better*. Perhaps I'm still not quite what I was as a carefree schoolgirl, but I'm *much better*. I can see the point of things again. I thought I'd tell you before we—'

Daniel started kissing his wife. A few moments later she managed to say, 'Darling – Leo's downstairs. We can't—'

'So he's downstairs, as he'd probably say.'

'But . . . he's a parson.'

'So am I.'

'But an American parson . . .'

In the end it was not so many minutes before Ruth was again ready to receive their guest. Leo put on a wonderful imitation of a man who understood completely the British custom whereby married couples always held a thorough private discussion of the weather before starting the evening. Nearly all the rest of that evening passed quickly and not over-memorably in the kind of semi-informative chatter to be expected of any new acquaintances with time to spare.

But not quite all of it. After Ruth had gone to bed, Leo gave some details of his acceptance of the Christian faith and of how this was connected with his renunciation of strong drink, and Daniel responded with some details of his own.

III

'If you want to know what it's called, you can read it off the label on the bottle,' said Eric Margolis. 'Remembering it afterwards, of course. Why they give these things such jawbreaking names beats me, unless for moral effect on the patient. If I put you on something called B-23 you may not be gripped enough, but if I say it's called chromopolyamineoxidase you're more likely to feel you're being properly looked after. And why not? But to answer your question: yes, this stuff is indeed reasonably new, in this country at least. They've had good results with it in the States and especially Australia, according to a man I know in Sydney who actually understands these matters. It's a narrow-spectrum deal; there are quite a few people it doesn't help at all, but those it does help it helps a lot. Ruth sounds as though she's one of the lucky ones.'

Eric's consulting room looked less like the traditional sort of consulting room than the drawing room of a small but posh hotel, with nothing overtly medical to be seen, not even a note-pad. Eric himself, a lanky person whose small mostly bald head was eked out with a dense beard, occupied an easy chair near a low table on which lay two or three novels in their jackets. Opposite him a similar chair held Daniel, sitting where he had sat on a couple of previous visits and assorted lunatics and neurotics on many times more. He said now, 'How long will she have to go on taking this stuff?'

'Some time. It's no use putting even an approximate date on it.'

'But there will be a date eventually, will there? Or will she be on it for the rest of her life?'

'That's most unlikely,' said Eric in his gentle voice, rubbing his fingertips together in the way he had, 'but at this stage I'm not ruling out anything.'

'But isn't there a danger she'll get addicted?'

'Addiction to a substance shows when somebody stops using that substance. Patients have come off this substance after a few weeks or a few years without serious trouble, as I told you. Some of them have felt funny or rotten for a while, which one can't discount, but nothing on the scale of a real drug hangover, like coming off, well, some popular tranquillisers and anti-depressives, which some have said is worse than what put them on it in the first place. Ruth stays on till it's all right for her to come off.'

'I see. How do we know when we've reached that stage?'

'We get some idea when we try a controlled reduction of the dose.'

'M'm. If you don't mind my saying so, Eric, it all sounds rather hit-or-miss to me.'

'That's how it is. More miss than hit, too, though fortunately things are getting better every year. About point-one of one per cent a year. The gloomy view of the situation is that we're no nearer understanding how these materials work than we were twenty years ago, so we've no way of telling which one will help which patient, and the consequence of that is we chop and change and keep our eyes and ears open for anything new that might be good.'

'Thank you, doctor,' said Daniel. 'Would there be a cheerful view?'

'No. But there is a slightly less gloomy one this time round. Let's say we have scored a hit with Ruth. That means there's something like an even chance she can be kept as she now is while in the meantime she gets better. A mental illness, if a prolonged bout of depression can be called that at all, is only like a physical illness in a couple of ways, but one of them is that its victims sometimes make a full recovery. Thank God.'

'What sort of long-term chance do you give Ruth at this stage?'

'More than evens, Daniel. Substantially more. With her intelligence and good temperament she's beginning to shape up as one of my successes. The last, what, *area* to count your chickens in is the mind, but . . . I won't say any more. Just, there's a good deal of hope where before there was only average hope, average hope being better than no hope at all but not much. Well, unless you've got anything more . . .'

Eric stood up. Daniel did the same, but said, 'Actually there is one other item, but could we talk about it somewhere else? What about that pub down on the corner?'

'Not there if you don't mind. They know me there because I take the occasional arachnophobe or homicidal maniac there. We'll try another place.'

On their way to it, Daniel asked, 'Don't you ever take notes of what a patient says?'

'No, I take a secret tape which I turn on and off with a secret switch. Better all round.'

'Did you turn it on for me?'

'I should say not. Tape costs money, you know. Sorry.'

'That's all right, only my nose does feel a little bit out of joint.'

Eric's other place was another pub, an extensive pub where, at this early hour, there was room to sit apart. By way of a token of decorum, a concealed apparatus quietly played one of the more understandably neglected of Handel's operas. Daniel brought Eric the gin and tonic he had asked for.

'Aren't you having anything at all?'

'I'm not thirsty.'

Daniel spoke with enough emphasis to make Eric glance at him but not pursue the matter. Soon afterwards Eric said, 'What was this item you were going to raise?'

'Oh yes. Well, it's a bit difficult to put neatly. More a feeling.'

'Some quite important points are that.'

'Yeah. Well . . . I'm afraid it rather brings in philosophical things. Things to do with belief. You know, church doctrine.'

'To me, you can say anything you like about that. It's one of the great advantages of me from your point of view. But try not to go too fast.'

'Right.' Daniel paused again, then nodded to himself. 'Right. For all your professional pessimism, you'd agree that more and more drugs are being discovered every day and the field of their application is widening all the time.'

'Yes. Exponentially.'

'Is there any theoretical limit to their expansion?'

'I don't quite know what you mean by that, but if it's, will there come a time when there are no more drugs to discover, then I haven't thought about it but it's certainly a long way off. If it's, are there going to turn out to be parts of the mind and human behaviour that can never be reached by drugs, then I have thought about that but to little effect. Actually theory doesn't help much there, because the question takes us outside pharmacology and biology and any other ology and into, what you said, philosophy, where I'm near enough at sea. But you want something more than that.' Eric poked inconclusively at the slice of lemon in his glass. Then he said rather quickly, 'Nothing I've learnt in the sense of being able to write it down, write it out, none of it tells me there are any areas of consciousness beyond the reach of human modification, and if the resulting prospect displeases you, don't investigate recent findings on the results of physical interferences with the brain by surgery or accident or both at once. As for gene surgery, I've made a personal point of not investigating that.'

'But,' said Daniel. 'At least I hope there's a but.'

'Oh, there is, beyond argument and beyond fact. Something tells me, and I mean tells me, not just suggests to me – something tells me that that is not so, that there is a part of each one of us no man could ever touch. I am I and you are you and will remain so. Unalterably. That something is very old, many times older than pharmacology. In my case it goes back at least as far as Abraham. In yours, Daniel,' said Eric gently, 'you'll allow me to say it's a little more recent than Abraham. But your personal . . . something . . . is stronger than mine. God has blessed you, my friend. I needn't tell you to be grateful for that.'

After a silence, Daniel said, 'I remember you telling me once that mad or disturbed people whose troubles disappear under the right chemotherapy, that some of them get to feel so well or at least so all right that they reckon they can manage without, and are back to square one in no time. Could anything like that happen to Ruth?'

'Ah. Well, since she's not in hospital there's nothing to stop her cutting her dosage down or even out. But if she does she'll soon start feeling rotten enough to go back on it off her own bat. Whereas . . .'

'Whereas if she doesn't feel rotten we could be starting to win.'

'We've won the first battle already, but yes. My turn to buy a drink. Another zero for you, or something more substantial?'

'I . . . Could I have a glass of water?'

'Water coming up.'

When Eric was back in his seat, Daniel said to him, 'Just to sum up, or put it another way: those domains of thought and action traditionally annexed to free will are being more and more encroached upon by the development of drugs and other novelties, and at present no end to this progression is foreseen. Sorry to sound so cut-and-dried, but it's the way I'm beginning to think these days. Have I left anything out?'

'But,' said Eric.

'I hadn't forgotten about but,' said Daniel.

'It's just that my Church is more easy-going than yours,' said Leo.

Daniel shook his head. 'That can't be true as things are today. Years ago it probably was.'

'Even now I doubt very much if your boys and girls would have scraped a helpless, hopeless drunk off the street and not only brought him back all the way but encouraged him, and I mean encouraged, not just put no obstacle in his way but positively begged him to take holy orders.'

'Well, that's an excellent description of what our lot did for me only a short time ago.'

'Oh, great. So here we are with another piece of our lives that's been pretty much the same for us both.'

'Part of us that's the same.'

'Pretty much the same.'

'Exactly the same.'

'Because we're exactly the same.'

'Exactly the same.'

Daniel felt comforted by the complete identity of himself with his twin and their complete accord in the matter. As before they sat in the kitchen, at the table. He turned his head away and looked out of the open garden door. Outside it was very bright and very still, with nearer objects in deep shade, paving stones and a stone tablet, evergreen plants and small shrubs in stone urns and earthenware pots, coils of dark-green hosepipe that had left dark puddles and patches of damp. The sight seemed to Daniel to reflect the tranquillity of his life. At the same time it occurred to him that he had not noticed the stone tablet before. He fancied it bore an inscription, but it was too far off for him to be certain of that, let alone to read whatever might have been there. He was about to get up and go and look when he heard a small sound from the far side of the table and turned back towards it.

A replica of himself was facing him. Ears, eyebrows, hair and its length and arrangement, shape of face, ears, everything was as Daniel was used to seeing it in the mirror, although he strongly suspected that that summary could not be true in fact.

'Who are you?' he asked curiously.

'It's hard to find a single word for who I am,' replied what he recognised as his own voice. 'Or what I am.

Nevertheless, if you and Leo are twins, you and he and I could be triplets. Quite conceivable, if you'll pardon the impropriety, vicar. As our brother recently explained to you, monozygotic twins come from a single fertilised ovum that has split into two. When one of those moieties splits again, we're presented with identical triplets and, as you may have read in various newspapers, there's no theoretical limit to the number of times that can happen, or be induced to happen. Are you with me so far, Daniel?'

'Yes.' Daniel might have added that what was being said to him was also to be heard, with total synchronicity, inside his head, but thought it advisable to keep quiet about that.

'Whatever their number,' resumed the being across the table, 'all the resulting persons or animals or vegetal entities are identical. The artificial process, known as cloning, has long been a botanical commonplace and one day, perhaps quite soon, may be practically as well as theoretically applicable to human beings. Compared with non-uniform organisms, clones offer an untold, unexplored range of advantages and possibilities. Some of these are of course social, even political, indicating a community as simple as an anthill or a beehive. But you and I, brother, aren't interested in that, in what may or may not actually happen in the future; our concern is philosophical and so timeless. When the uniqueness of the individual is found to be limited and finite, instead of universal and infinite, it ceases to be a usable concept. It follows that any ideas of free choice that may be nourished by a human unit, formerly known as an individual, are illusory and false. Your path to God, Daniel, was already there waiting for you. You had no alternative.'

The last few sentences had been audible only inside

Daniel's head, and when he looked up he was alone in the kitchen. Aware of nothing more than his need to do so, he got up and at his natural brisk pace walked out of the house by the garden door. He made for where he had seen the stone tablet, but could not find it. At the moment when he saw it was not there to be found, darkness closed about him. He stood still for a short time, then, for greater safety as he thought, dropped into a crouching position. What was under his hands and feet now was not stone but bare earth. The darkness that surrounded him was intense but not absolute; there was enough light from somewhere to show him that he was encircled by a flat, featureless plain that reached to the horizon in every direction. He felt that his spirit was leaving him.

Still in darkness, he became aware that he was breathing unusually: slowly in, sharply out, pause, then again. At the same time he found he was lying on something smoother and softer than earth.

'Are you awake?' said Ruth's voice quietly.

'Yes. Yes, I'm awake now.' In the time it took Daniel to utter these words his mind had altered what he had actually and inexpressibly dreamt into the dialogue or dialogues at his kitchen table and what had seemed to follow, and then in turn he had forgotten all that and was left with nothing but a strong, heavy feeling of loss and sorrow. 'I must have been dreaming,' he said. 'Did I wake you?'

'I was awake. Are you all right?'

'Oh yes. Oh yes, I'm all right now.'

But he must have said it wrong, because she at once switched on her bedside light, came over and knelt down by him and took his hands. 'Was it a very horrible dream?'

'It was rather.'

'But it's all over now, darling. Let's go down to the kitchen and have a cup of tea.'

'Not there, not for me,' said Daniel in a rush.

Ruth glanced at him for a moment. 'All right, you stay here and relax. Don't you dare go to sleep again.'

'I won't, I promise I won't.'

'I'll be very quick,' she said after another pause.

Alone in his workroom a minute later, Daniel knelt down by his desk and started to pray. He thanked God for preserving him from whatever had seemed to threaten him as he slept and for taking from him all memory of it. Then he stopped, stopped the silent recital of words which was his habitual form of prayer in private. Always before, God had been listening to his prayers, or he, Daniel, had believed unquestioningly that that was so, which no doubt came to the same thing. Now, he found he could not believe that his words were going anywhere. But he went on silently forming them in his mind, this time ones that asked for help.

None had arrived by the time he heard Ruth approaching with the tea-tray. He went and sat on his desk-chair, then got up again and helped her set out the tea-things on the corner of the desk he kept clear for such arrangements. She pulled up her chair and sent him a look of great friendliness.

'You haven't been yourself since that night you and Leo sat up talking, have you?'

'No, I haven't,' he agreed.

'And this dream you had is more of the same.'

'It feels like that. In effect, yes.'

After a moment, she said, 'You'll have to tell me sooner or later, you know. And no, you're not keeping me up.'

'It's painful,' said Daniel.

'Yes. But I'm here.'

'Can I have some more tea?' When this was done, he went on, 'That night, Leo and I went over our lives in detail, starting as far back as we could remember, childhood friends, childhood ailments, schooldays, school friends, girls, university, first job, all that. Until we were in our middle twenties or so it was, well, let's call it reassuringly boring. Quite a number of resemblances, such as both of us having a close friend at college called Paul, both of us liking *The Tempest* best of Shakespeare's plays and thinking Horatio had more in him than Hamlet, but nothing on the scale of those twin brothers he told us about who had both independently had a seat built round a tree in their garden, nothing where anybody who heard of it wouldn't think it was a bit of a coincidence and that was about that, nothing *spooky*. In fact, as we went on I started to feel I was going to get away with it, I started to feel safe. Meaning, as you saw from the very beginning, I was afraid of Leo, not as a person but because of what he was, what he is. And I was dead right to be afraid of him, or at least to wish more than anything that he had never existed.

'I dare say I felt a twinge or two of a rather different sort when we got on to you, that's to say when I got on to you and he got on to his Ruth. But the first part of it was all right, in fact it was, well, pleasant to go over our early times and sort of relaxing to find they were rather like theirs, which you'd have expected with two very similar men in pretty similar circumstances and countries. I thought there might be trouble of one sort or another when, I forget which one of us it was, but something was said that could have led to us letting on about, you know, personal things, private things. I closed up straight away, which was probably me being English again, but then he did the same thing, so perhaps Americans have their own scale of things to keep quiet about that isn't so different from ours. Or perhaps that's just how Leo is. After all, we are twins.'

So far Daniel had spoken in an equable, controlled way that was still not natural to him and included pauses in odd places. By now he was sitting hand in hand with Ruth, who had listened without any sign of wanting to speak. Soon he went on as before.

'I'd better come to the crunch, my love. When you start talking about boozing, serious boozing, you find there isn't a lot to say. For reasons you don't understand and can't be bothered with, it suddenly dawns on you that you've got to be drunk and you set about getting there by the nearest available means. You don't enjoy getting there or anything else about it, that's not the idea at all. So there you are, drunk, and that's that. The rest is a matter of falling over, throwing up, stealing, fighting, waking up on a train you don't remember thinking about catching, let alone getting on to, being locked in a police cell and, if you're not so lucky, an epileptic fit or two to see you back to square one. Plus some other people's chatter about tension and in-security and feelings of inadequacy. All serious drunks are the same, except over details that can be mildly interesting, such as brainy places to hide a bottle.

'Some people seem to get out of it on their own. I'd never have managed it like that. Then one morning I woke up lying on my bed fully dressed, doing pretty well for that time of day, in fact. But I had nothing to drink and no money, so I realised I was going to have to go out and walk some distance to the off-licence to pick up two four-packs of large cans of Aalborg Original Brew and charge them to the brother of a mate of mine. Then I suddenly thought to myself I didn't want to do anything like that ever again, and if I could get some support or some sign from somewhere that there was the slightest chance that I wouldn't, then I'd really try not to, and I couldn't understand it then and even after all this time I still don't completely, but I managed to get down on my knees and pray. I'm still not sure what made me. I've never told you or anyone else this before, and there's not a lot of it I could tell anyone, but after half an hour I knew I had a personal understanding with JC that said that as long as I went on really trying he'd see me right. And he did. I can't say much more than that, except perhaps, if I can get it across, it was a special, one-off agreement between him and me, run up for the occasion, absolutely not any kind of standard contract. I think that probably gets it as far as it goes.

'So you can imagine how I felt when Leo told me about the arrangement he'd had with JC and it was exactly the same as mine, so exactly the same that I could tell what he was going to say next and I could have said the ends of his sentences with him, word for word. So my special understanding hadn't been special after all, I'd just been hearing about another of the same and if there was one then why not half a dozen or a million others? A standard contract, you see, maybe different in inessentials but the same in essentials; anyone with the correct set of genes will do to accept it, so *I* wasn't special after all either. But I wanted to think I was special, not because I was Daniel Davidson but because I was me, I was unique, I was an individual. But I'd just found out I wasn't an – I've said it already. So what was I?

'But Leo was delighted. It was what he'd been hoping for from the beginning, what he'd meant when he said he hadn't come all this way just to compare notes with me. For Leo, it was a kind of final proof of God's greatness, that in the universe he made there could be two or more things that were unique and identical at the same time. But God as I see him could never be as great as that, because he's bound by the laws of reason.'

Daniel looked into Ruth's face and saw in it hope, trust and fear, and lowered his gaze. He went on at the same even pace.

'There was an old Church saying that God would never let a Christian soul escape from him. It might wander to the ends of creation, but he would bring it back to him with a mere twitch on the thread. Whoever came up with that was probably thinking of something like a fishing-line, but to me God's thread has turned out to be the sort that controls the movements of a puppet. But whatever happens I'll always be grateful to him, because he sent me you.'

Ruth was crying. 'I wish I could believe,' she said.

'So do I, my love. Now what do you say to both of us going down to the kitchen and making some fresh tea?'

'I say yes.'

'Thank you for not saying anything while I was maundering on.'

'Daniel, you and I know it wasn't maundering.'

'Sorry.'

'At any rate, now I know why Leo went off in such a rush.'

'He had a lot to get back for. And his trip had served its purpose.'

Some weeks later, Daniel was saying to Greg Macdonald, 'You mean you do want another piece from me, is that what you're saying?'

'Well, yes, of course, I'd like to see anything you write, Daniel.'

'Ah, but excuse me, excuse me, but that's not quite the same thing, is it? You might *like to see* something I'd written, perhaps you would, and then again perhaps you wouldn't, but I was talking about me writing something for the *paper*. How about that, eh?'

'Okay, fine, fine with me, but what subject were you thinking of?'

'Listen, I'm a great believer in never doing a single stroke of work, however small, until either I've been paid for it or unless I've been promised payment, and thinking of a subject is work, right? As soon as you commission me, I'll make a start on thinking of a subject, as soon as you commission me.'

'All right then, Daniel. A piece of the usual length at the usual rates. Good.'

'What about an advance?'

After almost no hesitation Macdonald brought out his wallet, and after only a little more hesitation took from it a twenty-pound note. Daniel soon put down the glass he had been holding and had also been glancing at from time to time with great seriousness. This done, he set about ceremoniously stowing away his advance in his own wallet, but halfway through this operation the note slipped from his fingers and sideslipped to the floor. First holding up a hand to forestall any intervention from Macdonald, he retrieved the note successfully enough but not at all speedily. The performance drew laughter from near by, only a little but sufficient to cause Daniel to go and remonstrate with a group at the bar that included the urchin-like assistant editor and the stately astrologer. They were soon joined by the landlord of the Sussex, and then almost at once Daniel strolled back to where Macdonald stood, glancing condescendingly from side to side as he came.

'This place has gone down a lot,' he said.

Whatever hope Macdonald might have had of a word or two of thanks for somebody's generosity with money could clearly be abandoned. He said with a bright smile, 'Any first thoughts on a subject?'

Daniel, whose expression had grown abstracted in the

past few seconds, frowned a little. 'M'm?' he asked with some impatience.

'You know, for your piece. Any ideas?'

'Oh for Christ's sake,' said Daniel, still with impatience rather than anger, 'what are you burbling about? All this . . . If you've got anything to say why don't you say it out in the open, for Christ's sake.'

'I was just wondering if there was anything special you felt like writing about for the paper.'

'Oh, that.' Now Daniel sounded contemptuous. Having said as much, he seemed at rather a loss, but soon rallied. 'If you're hoping for something about something like thoughts on stopping being a bloody parson, you're wrong.'

'I wasn't—'

'For one thing, you can't ever stop being a bloody parson once you are one. It's called being ordained. Ha! You're it for life, er, old boy, and I'm not going to write about that. For one thing,' he explained, 'it would be . . . bad form. I told the bishop so. Too private, I told him. Now let's have the same again. My turn.'

Daniel gave a grunt of pleased surprise at finding he had a twenty-pound note about him. His mood changed when the barman turned out to be reluctant to serve him. The landlord reappeared. Macdonald went out into the passage and activated the telephone there.

'Ruth?' he said a moment later. 'It's Mac. Yeah, in the Sussex. No, I didn't, he just came walking in here just a few minutes ago. Yes, I'm afraid he is. Not so far, but I'd say any moment. Okay now, I'll hang on till you get here. Ah, not at all.'

On his way back, Macdonald heard a confused shouting from the bar.

Note: Further information about identical or monozygotic

113

twins can be found in Twins, by Peter Watson (Hutchinson, 1981), among other places. I haveselected from Watson's account of pairs of such twins who have been separated soon after birth and brought up apart. Further details of the male twins Leo describes (James Lewis and James Springer, born in Piqua, Ohio, USA in 1939) and of the female twins (Irene Reid and Jeanette Hamilton, born in UK in 1944) are given on pp. 9–11 and pp. 49–52 of Twins.

A research group to study the subject was set up under Professor Thomas Bouchard at the University of Minnesota in 1971.

Toil and Trouble

I

Adrian Hollies was a literary agent, which is to say he was a director of a prosperous firm of such, Parkes & Richards Ltd of Princess Square, WC2. One afternoon in early May he was sitting in his office in their offices talking to a well-known senior client of the firm, the novelist Jack Brownlow. Or rather Brownlow, enjoying the advantage of his valued seniority, was mostly talking to Adrian. In fact at the moment he was asking him one of those questions that no successful literary agent really enjoys being asked.

'What's your honest opinion, Adrian? I mean, I take it you have read the whole thing.'

'Of course, Jack. Well, for what it's worth, I think it shows you at the top of your form. Er, that is the character of Tom and his extraordinary relationship with Sonia, not to speak of the affair with Amanda, especially the part where they all find themselves—'

'Because unless you feel quite wholehearted about it I think I ought to find someone who does to represent me. I'm not trying to hold a pistol to your head.'

Much, said Adrian to himself. Out loud he said, 'I haven't the slightest reservation. I've never been in any doubt about the quality of your work.' The second part of that was not quite true. At least twice in his nineteen years with Parkes & Richards it had crossed his mind, albeit without lingering there, that against appearances there might be something to be said for Jack's work. After all, the first novel back in 1958 had been quite readable for a global best seller.

'One of the young fellows at Fortuitous Millennium,' said Brownlow now, 'was telling me they'd give me substantially better paperback terms there than what you managed to get me for my last one.'

'Was that Mark Skinner?'

Brownlow hesitated. 'Could have been, but I never really caught the name properly.'

'I think at your time of life, Jack, you'd do well to consider the advantages of sticking to the devil you know.'

The devil Brownlow knew, a small firm specialising chiefly in military history and reminiscences, had had the luck to publish that runaway success of 1958, and continued to publish him now he broke a little better or a little worse than even with his chronicles of elderly daydreams. To be sure, he was still something of a name, a quality that also helped to account for his continuance in the Parkes & Richards string. But both publisher and agent were also unwilling, out of compassion or cowardice, to bring him up against the fact that at the age of sixty-three he had ceased for ever to be the kind of literary property he had once been.

Brownlow had at any rate not cared for the last remark, had possibly sensed something of what lay behind it, but he had hardly begun the long process of asking for clarification when a nearby telephone purred. Adrian snatched it up with simulated annoyance.

'Yes. Yes, Tania. Oh, not again. How long ago? Well, I don't remember meeting him. Oh yes. All right.' In the next ten seconds Adrian got his face to run quickly through some of its less welcoming expressions. 'Mr Pennistone? No, that's all right. Well, if I said anything at all I meant it, including that. No, I remember it well. Your book is *unpublishable*, and when I say unpublishable I know what I'm . . . I'm sorry, but I happen to have *Jack Brownlow* with me at the moment, so perhaps you'll understand if I . . . Very well, if you say so. Of course.' Clunk.

However this performance might have affected the unlucky Pennistone, it worked wonders for Brownlow, who did nothing more than extract from Adrian a promise to spend some thought and research on the possibility of a change of publisher, with special reference to an improved paperback deal. So all was as well as it could be.

'Can I see you put it in?' asked Brownlow finally.

This question surprised Adrian less than it might have done because he had heard it in these circumstances before. What was to be put in was the xeroxed typescript Brownlow had brought with him, and what this was to be put into was the firm's vaults for safekeeping.

'It's silly of me,' he said without encountering any opposition, 'but until that's done I can't help worrying that some joker might steal my only copy. Now there's one in here too I don't care if my house burns down. Most authors have their funny little ways and I suppose that's mine.'

After Brownlow had gone, Adrian thought for a time about him and his funny little way. It could be taken as showing a relentless determination to stay in touch with the reading public, a group seldom far from his thoughts, or just to continue to be counted as a writer. That was understandable enough in somebody with his history, but even total non-starters like Pennistone had their version of it. What was it about the almost always frustrating career of authorship that made them pursue it so obstinately, in the face of every disappointment and discouragement? By rights Brownlow would have packed it in a couple of books ago, decided to live on his fat, taken to drink, fallen down dead, even found something else to occupy him, but no, he was hellbent on going on writing his very own sort of terrible novel *and getting it published.*

At this point in his reflections, Adrian almost literally bumped into Derek Richards coming out of his office. Derek was the son of the co-founder of the firm and was widely said to owe his position in it to little but his paternity. Perhaps in compensation, he affected a wild-eyed, bardic manner that suggested a mind usually bent on higher things than representing writers. Nevertheless there was a kind of distant friendliness about him.

'You managed to get rid of that old fart Brownlow, then,' he said.

'Unfortunately he left the typescript of a new novel with us.'

'Why can't he go back to his roots in where is it and stay there?'

'Bristol. I suppose he wants to feel he's still a writer.'

'You mean there was a time when he was one?'

'Enough people would say so and there must be some who'd say he still is.'

They crossed the entrance hall of the building. Derek said with an air of indifference, 'Yes, I've noticed that you literary agent fellows tend to, what's the word, *identify* with your clients. Now and then to a rather touching degree.'

'Maybe. You should hear what we think about the likes of Brownlow in our innermost thoughts.'

'But I trust you're not going to tell me.'

'Haven't you ever wished you were a writer, Derek?'

'Never, thank God. You have, I know. Be very careful that nothing happens to you, or you may find yourself writing it up.'

'Don't worry, nothing's going to happen to me.'

But evidently Derek was tired of the subject of writers and writing. 'So Keith Gordon has eluded both the arm of the law and the assassin's bullet,' he said.

'What? What are you talking about?'

'I got it on the News. A chunk of masonry squashed the conniving villain as he was about to enter his offices in the City. Apparently an accident.'

'Surely not. There must be hundreds of poor swindled sods dying to knock off an arch-shit like Thief Gordon. What were the circumstances?'

'You obviously wouldn't expect me to know all of them, but evidently there were plenty. So far they hadn't managed to find any suspicious ones. What seems to have happened . . .'

And for the rest of their short walk to the pub that was their undeclared destination, Adrian discussed with Derek the fate of the famously shady financier, and the very existence of Jack Brownlow altogether faded from his mind.

II

A couple of mornings later, Adrian was preparing to leave his comfortable Tufnell Park flat and go to work when the telephone rang. The girl he lived with, a picture researcher called Julie something, answered it.

'It's for you,' she told Adrian, chewing a croissant.

'Mr Hollies? Oh, it's Sergeant Chatterton here, sir, Metropolitan Police, Kilburn Division,' said a reliable youngish voice, which went on to elicit his agreement that he was the owner of a specified car. This part took place against a considerable distant accompaniment of ringing telephones, buzzing buzzers and general intra-mural clamour. The voice continued, 'We picked up the vehicle in question early this morning, sir. It had been malparked near—'

'I had no idea, I didn't even know it had gone,' said Adrian in a state of some consternation.

'No doubt you didn't, sir. We have good reason to believe it had been used in an attempted break-in at some premises in Maida Vale last night. I wonder, sir, if we were to send one of our cars to pick you up, if you'd be good enough to come and collect it, bringing with you the relevant documents just to formally establish owner-ship. We'll get a car up to you right away.'

Not more than twenty minutes later a white car with an orange stripe round it, labelled Police, duly pulled up outside the flat. Adrian picked up the required pieces of paper and looked about for Julie to kiss her goodbye for the day, but she had already left. Outside on the pavement he was greeted by a red-faced, solid-looking man in his middle thirties and a pale, taller, younger one. Both wore smart police uniform with peaked caps.

'Mr Hollies?' said the older policeman. 'Good of you to be with us so promptly, sir. I'm PC Beaumont-Snaith and this is PC Llewelyn. This business must have come as something of a shock to you, sir, but don't you worry, it'll all be settled very shortly.'

With some vague idea of verification, Adrian said, 'I was rather expecting somebody called Sergeant Chatterton.'

'Ah, he'll be down at the station waiting for you, sir. I'm afraid poor old Chatty is a bit on the desk-bound side these days, eh, Taff?'

'Oh, indeed,' said Llewelyn with a chuckle.

'If you wouldn't mind getting in the back, Mr Hollies? Rather a squash, I'm afraid, but this week we're having to take one of our trainees with us everywhere we go. Chris, this is Mr Hollies. DC Fotheringay.'

'You're a detective, then,' said Adrian alertly to the large man in plain clothes as he settled himself next to him in the back of the car. He heard Llewelyn say something into a hand-microphone about returning to base.

'I'll tell you all about that, sir,' said the large man in a deep voice, 'if you wouldn't mind just picking up that file for me down there on the floor. It's a bit further than I like to bend, I'm afraid.'

'Of course.'

Adrian's fingers had not quite touched the grey cardboard oblong on the floor in front of him when a strong hand fastened on the back of his neck and propelled him bodily downwards. A sharp point penetrated the skin of his upper arm through jacket and shirtsleeve and, before fear could reach him, he felt himself floating into a region where there were no policemen and no car nor anything else in particular.

After a lapse of time impossible to measure, Adrian became aware that he was lying on rather than in a bed that was strange to him. By degrees he found that this bed stood in an equally unfamiliar, small, clean but barely furnished room. The light was dim but definite enough for him to be sure it came from some artificial source and not from the two windows, which were heavily curtained and, as he was to find later, blacked out with thick paint. At any rate, he had no difficulty in reading the few words typed on a sheet of paper he found on the bedside table beside an electric bell-push with wires affixed. The message ran, 'Don't try to get out. You won't make it.'

Adrian found that he was still dressed as he had been, apart from his shoes, tie and jacket, which proved to be

121

ready to hand. There were two doors out of the room, the main one strongly and invisibly fastened, the other open and leading to a proportionately small bathroom with wc, handbasin, shower, comb, soap and towels, all in good order. No razor, in fact nothing more. Adrian peed, washed his hands and face and combed his hair. On returning to the bedroom, he investigated a previously unregarded table near the main window. Under a white cloth it bore a plate of cheese sandwiches and a flask of whisky. Without premeditation he disposed of both and found them excellent. Then he put on shoes, tie and jacket again, pressed the bell-push and sat down on a padded chair facing the main door. Within a minute it opened and in came the two men Adrian knew as Beaumont-Snaith and Fotheringay. Both had changed out of their former clothes into cotton sweaters and denims. Their manner had ceased to be respectful without becoming hostile in any way.

'How are you feeling, Hollies?' asked Fotheringay in his bass voice. He perched quite companionably on the end of the bed while Beaumont-Snaith leant against the wall by the door.

'A bit heavy,' said Adrian. 'Sort of limp. I think perhaps I'm still dozy from that stuff you pumped into me. What was it?'

Fotheringay looked at Beaumont-Snaith, who told him not to do that and added, 'I just took what was given me and passed it on to you as ordered.'

After nodding resignedly, Fotheringay said to Adrian, 'Well, the next bit of orders is we take you along to talk to, er, the next one up from us, if you reckon you're ready for it. There's no great rush.'

'Oh good. But I'm ready for it.'

'Oh, yeah.' The big man made no move. 'Aren't you afraid, Hollies?'

'Naturally I am, but ever since I woke up about twenty minutes ago I've had a lot to think about, for instance what this place is and what I'm supposed to be doing here. Or rather what the chap you've mistaken me for would have been doing here.'

'Oh, so you reckon you've been mistaken for somebody else.'

'I know I must have been.'

Over by the door, Beaumont-Snaith pushed himself upright. 'I think it's time we fetched you along to meet the next one up from us, don't you, er, Fotheringay?'

Their way took them along an L-shaped piece of carpeted corridor in which and from which there was nothing to be seen and, except for the burble of distant traffic, nothing to be heard. All the same, Adrian sensed he was on an upper floor of a considerable building that stood on its own. Beaumont-Snaith, in the lead, knocked at a closed door and entered, followed by the other two.

A well-groomed, well-dressed man of about forty, who had been sitting behind a large desk writing something, put down his pen and took off his spectacles with an exclamation of pleasure, rose to his feet and extended a hand. 'Good morning, Mr Hollies,' he said affably, in decisive tones that seemed to Adrian in some way familiar. 'Do take a seat. So glad you could come.'

Without volition, Adrian shook the proffered hand and almost as spontaneously took the seat, a comfortable chair near and at an angle to the desk. He hardly needed to glance at the heavy furniture, the rows of books and periodicals or the Italian prints on the walls to perceive the ambience aimed at as expensive-professional. Beaumont-Snaith and Fotheringay were no longer to be seen.

'At this stage of the proceedings,' said the man behind the desk, smiling, 'I should of course press a switch and tell somebody offstage that I don't want any calls or visitors till further notice, which is acknowledged by the appallingly distorted voice of the somebody, but that would be going a little too far. Still, there is a switch I can press to cause something amusing to happen.'

No switch sounded, but after a moment sounds of ringing telephones, buzzing buzzers and the like were to be heard from a concealed loudspeaker or speakers. With another smile, this time an eager, guileless, almost childish one that might have heralded the repetition of some established old favourite, the unknown recited carefully against this background, 'Mr Hollies? Oh, it's Sergeant Chatterton here, sir, Metropolitan Police, Kilburn Division. I wonder if you'd mind confirming that you're the owner of,' and vehicular details followed. In the middle of them the loudspeakers faded. 'There, now. What do you think of that, eh?'

'I think that whatever it is you're trying to do here you're doing it to the wrong man.'

'Oh, the *wrong man*. I see. But I'm afraid that's quite impossible, Mr Hollies. Well, let's just check, shall we? Here we are – Adrian Hugo Hollies, born younger son of Frederick Irving Hollies deceased and Diana Victoria *née* Barton, educated Westminster School and Trinity College, Oxford, blah blah *blah*, at present director of Parkes & Richards, et cetera. Oh yes. Er, current live-in girlfriend Julie Scharwenka, employed by Central Magazines plc. That is your life, isn't it . . . Mr Hollies?'

'Yes, but I still say all this couldn't possibly have been meant for me and there's still been a mistake, it must just have happened at an earlier stage, for heaven's sake. Surely.'

'Oh dear, I'm sorry to say that's not the case either,' continued Chatterton's voice for a moment before an abrupt return to the earlier stockbroking inflection.

'You'll have to take my word for that, my dear fellow. I was present when this thing was set up and you, Adrian Hugo Hollies of Parkes & Richards, were at the centre of the picture right from the beginning.'

'Oh. What is this *thing* you mention?'

'You know some of the answer to that already. A mechanism for removing you from your daily life and imprisoning you for an indefinite period somewhere you'll never escape or be rescued from.'

This silenced Adrian, but only for a moment. 'Is that all?'

'It's what you might have inferred unassisted. Some of the rest is that your experience here is an end in itself. Nothing is required of you in the shape of information, your signature to a confession or any other action or reaction. Whatever happens you stay. Yes?'

'I was going to ask, though why I should hope to get anything helpful out of you I don't really know, I was going to ask if this is supposed to be a punishment for something I've done.'

The man Adrian was always to think of as Chatterton shook his head. It was a rather handsome head, in fact his whole being radiated something like distinction. 'No,' he said firmly. 'I'll tell you what is true, that indeed you have done something that displeased somebody, but to tell you what it is or was would be to immediately forfeit the anonymity that is of the essence of this enterprise, and . . . and after all, punishment suffered without knowledge of either the offence or the offended party can hardly be called punishment at all. So, let's call it revenge. Somebody intends to satisfy himself – or herself – by retaliating upon your person for some wrong you've inflicted upon him or her.' Chatterton appeared less than pleased with this formulation, but after a pause continued fluently enough, 'And that satisfaction and that wrong correspond to no legal definition, otherwise my principal would no doubt have looked for redress through the courts.' He finished strongly and with an air of triumph, smiling as he spoke and springily adjusting his position behind the desk.

'You mean any sensible person would think that whatever it is I'm meant to have done is ridiculously disproportionate to all this elaborate and obviously very expensive bloody *fuss*.'

Chatterton looked wary. 'I'm sorry, Mr Hollies, I'm not sure I follow you.'

'Really? Well, just consider. I'm a literary agent and as such I must have inflicted a great many wrongs on people, or what they might see as wrongs. And in my private life I've done quite a few things I'm ashamed of, like many of us. But nothing on this *scale*. Unless your principal is mad. Well, is he? Or is she?'

The question seemed to flummox Chatterton a little. 'I'm afraid I can't answer that. Or rather, I can assure you between ourselves that for practical purposes he or she is . . . is entirely sane.'

'Have I injured you?' asked Adrian quickly.

'Oh no, Mr Hollies, you've never done anything to me, anything at all. Why, you've never set eyes on me before, have you?' For a moment there, the shadowy presence of Sergeant Chatterton, and the absence of Chatterton QC or FRCS, was unmistakable. 'You and I have no quarrel.'

'So how much does this carry?'

But this time upmarket Chatterton was prepared. 'The organisation will naturally see to it that I don't lose by this interruption of my more regular activities.'

'Such as resting, eh?' When this brought no reply but a huffy toss of the head, Adrian went on, 'How long do you expect this interruption to last?'

'That's easy,' said Chatterton with a less pleasant smile than before. 'As long as it takes.'

'As long as what takes? As long as it takes to what?'

'We have a modest programme arranged for you, Mr Hollies, but I'm afraid it would be premature at this stage to speculate on its likely duration. It'll last quite long enough to satisfy you, you'll find.' The last part was delivered in a tone that seemed to lack some of the required conviction.

'I see. I mean I see I'm not going to get anything out of you if you can help it. Why did you have me fetched along here, to this room?'

'If you really want to know, removing any unhelpful theories you might have formed about the reason for your presence here, impressing you with—'

'But leaving a big question mark over the disparity between size of punishment and crime.'

'From our point of view there's nothing unhelpful about question marks being left in your mind,' said Chatterton with some complacency. After a pause he added in a different tone, 'And I wanted to have a look at you.'

'I hope the sight's been worth the trouble.'

'Aren't you frightened, Mr Hollies?'

'One of your underlings asked me that. I told him of course I was, but I was trying not to let it interfere with my powers of observation and thought.'

'Admirable. If true.' Chatterton paused again before hurrying on, 'I've got news for you, Hollies. You won't be done any physical harm. Nothing actually painful's going to happen to you, nothing . . . *messy*, you understand?' Then, with yet another change of mood or idiom, he continued, 'But before this is over you're going to wish that all you had to put up with was something along those lines, something painful in that way, something that really . . . *hurts*. Right, I've said enough already. Ah, here we are.'

A door opened and the man earlier called PC Llewelyn, no doubt summoned a few moments before, came into the room. He entered in a lounging, rolling fashion before a kind of military yelp from Chatterton smartened him up in an instant. Coming to something like a posture of attention he said loudly, 'Yes, sir.'

'Wake up, Llewelyn.'

'I'm sorry, sir, truly I am.' This was said in a noticeable Welsh accent. The fellow had taken his jacket off but still wore his uniform trousers. Although there seemed to be no other definable change in his appearance, he looked uncommonly scruffy.

'Convey Mr Hollies back to his room and secure the door.'

'Right, sir.' Llewelyn at any rate spoke sharply.

Adrian looked from one to the other of the two as they went through their performance. His expression evidently offended Chatterton, who gave him a curt nod of dismissal and gestured impatiently to Llewelyn to remove him.

His return trip along the corridor was less smooth than the outward journey. Scruffy or not, Llewelyn was quite strong, and provided unnecessary encouragement to continue to move by means of a hand clamped on his upper arm. The door of the room he had woken up in was ajar and Llewelyn's hand propelled him across the threshold. Before the door could be shut Adrian said clearly,

'The devil damn thee black, thou cream-faced loon!'

Llewelyn stared back at him with a look of puzzlement, surprise, dismay or of all three, but for a moment he neither spoke nor moved.

'Whom we invite to see us crowned at Scone.'

At this, Llewelyn scowled ferociously and gave
Adrian a push in the chest forceful enough to send him
staggering and almost falling. When he had recovered
himself the door was shut and, he soon discovered,
fastened. His instinct was for setting about getting it
open again, but he had no way of doing so, certainly no
quick or non-noisy way. No such decisive move would
in any case make sense without knowledge of where he
might find an exit from the house. And a means of using
it. If any. It looked as if he might as well heed the advice
he had received on waking, that he would not escape by
his own efforts.

The scrap of paper bearing this message was no longer
to be found. The remains of his snack had likewise been
cleared away. The bed had been remade. A more
thorough look than he had earlier ventured showed him
pyjamas, fresh underclothes, shirts. Their mundane
practicality seemed designed to dishearten him. With
head bent he moved slowly round the room a couple of
times, then halted and for some minutes stared at the wall
in an unfocused manner. After that he sat down on the
bed and paused a moment before dropping his head into
his hands and rocking slowly to and fro. Anyone looking
at him would have said that a thoroughly wretched man,
if not a despairing one, was sitting there. Presently
Adrian drew his legs up on to the bed and lay down on his
side with his knees drawn up and his hands clasped.
Unexpectedly, he slept.

There passed another immeasurable tract of time. At
its end, at the sound of the door being unlocked, Adrian
sprang up and stood beside the bed, smoothing his hair
and straightening his tie. When all four of the men he had
previously seen came into the room, they found him
facing them in a posture of defiance.

After sending him a look of peculiar distaste,

Chatterton moved over to one side, as if to underline his supervisory status. 'Come along, Hollies,' he said sharply.

Fotheringay and Llewelyn began to move forward, but Adrian eluded their grasp. 'Let me come of my own accord, please. I'm quite capable of setting one foot in front of the other.'

'Oh, good show, sir,' said Fotheringay, 'but anybody can see you're terrified. Why not admit it?'

'What, terrified of you?'

Fotheringay's immediate response was to punch Adrian in the stomach. He collapsed on to the bed. 'That was quite unnecessary,' said someone: Chatterton.

'Just a tap, that's all. Look, he's getting up already.'

'Our orders are not to hurt him physically.'

'There won't be a mark on him, if that's what's bothering you.'

By now Adrian was facing them again, still panting and groaning, half doubled up, but back on his feet, and was allowed to make his own way out of the bedroom, round a couple of corners in the passage and into a room of about the same size but partly subdivided by a grey-painted screen on rollers. Two men were visible: after a first glance one of them went behind the screen and the other led an unresisting Adrian over to a corner where there stood a narrow backless couch of the sort to be met with in doctors' consulting rooms.

'Take off your jacket and shirt and then get up on here, please.'

Adrian followed instructions and successively had his blood pressure taken and allowed auscultation of his chest. Both exercises were rapid but thorough.

'Now sit up and take a series of deep breaths as I tell you, please.'

He felt the small cool circle of the stethoscope applied in turn to various parts of his back.

'Thank you. Please get dressed and sit on the chair.'

'Well?' asked another voice.

'His heart and circulation appear excellent. His blood pressure is above normal, but then he's obviously in a condition of extreme tension, if only as shown by his respiratory rate.'

'So there's no real risk?'

'In an undertaking of this kind there's *always* a risk, but if you mean am I prepared to take this risk then yes, I am.'

'Good. Let's get on with it, then.'

'Mr Hollies? Mr Hollies, I'm going to put you to sleep for a couple of minutes, nothing more than that. When you wake up you'll be in one piece and still here. Do you understand? Oh well, here goes.'

When Adrian came to himself after what he suspected to be only a short time, he was in some discomfort. He had been strapped into a chair in a way that prevented him from leaving it and also bound his wrists to its arms. More noticeably, his head was tightly clamped and what felt like pieces of sticky tape had been applied to his eyelids to prevent even their slight closure. A large screen of the TV type, at present blank, filled most of his vision. He must have made some movement because almost at once a voice spoke to him from behind his chair, the voice of the man who had seemed to be some sort of doctor.

'How are you feeling?'

'Restricted.'

'No nausea or trouble with breathing?'

'I've never felt better in my life.'

'Bravely spoken, Mr Hollies. Happy viewing.'

As he spoke, a thrumming click sounded, the screen in front of Adrian lit up and in a moment, with excellent definition and lifelike colour, images began to appear. The first of these, that of an attractive young woman,

Adrian found pleasant enough, and he had no objection when, smiling at the camera, she proceeded to undress, nor did he find what immediately followed any worse than embarrassing. When other persons joined her, however, he very quickly started showing signs of discomfort and not long after of distress. When a cry of pain sounded from the direction of the screen, he struggled to free himself and to turn his head away. Within a couple of minutes he was making anguished sounds and, as far as was possible to him, thrashing about. A female scream of terror and his own scream rose together, at which point the film froze and two or more men seized him and gagged him. But as soon as the coloured shapes were again in motion and appropriate sounds to be heard, he was able to show how much clamour could be created by a gagged man, especially in the forms of shrieks and inarticulate noises of protest and pain. In the end the man who had last spoken hurried forward and, with the screen now darkened, silence fell.

This time Adrian woke up lying on his bed. His eyelids were sore, his eyes ached and his lower lip was swollen and tender; he remembered biting it and feeling blood trickle down his chin. Despite these things he felt comfortable and languid, and guessed he was under some sedative or painkiller. He was alone. Presently, taking his time, he pushed himself upright and round until he was sitting on the edge of the bed. He had not long to wait.

The door clicked a couple of times and opened to admit the supposed doctor, who was now wearing a suit and tie. He looked closely at Adrian and said, 'You should be lying down.'

'I can get all the rest I want. I'm not going anywhere.'

The doctor was not listening. He brought from his jacket two small containers and handed them over. 'Take two of the round red ones to stop things hurting, not more than six in twenty-four hours. The white ones will calm you down and also help you to sleep. Dose of two, maximum six a day, got it?'

'Are you off somewhere?'

'I have things to see to.'

When the doctor had gone, Adrian went into the bathroom and came back holding a glass of water. Before he could have taken a pill there was the unexpected sound of a tap on the outside of his door.

'Come in,' he called. At the sight of Chatterton and Fotheringay he got up not very steadily, seized a chair by the back and ran at them with it, calling to them to keep their hands off him.

Fortheringay twisted the chair out of his grasp. 'Sit down, Mr Hollies,' he said easily.

As he sat on the bed again, Adrian said, 'Will you tell me something? Please?'

'Maybe.'

'Those, those things you made me see, they weren't real, were they?'

'Well . . .'

'When those men, when they forced the girl to do what she did, that wasn't really happening, was it? Please tell me.'

'We weren't on that side of it, Chatterton and me.'

'I mean, when they started . . . started . . . that poor girl,' said Adrian, and burst into tears, racking sobs he seemed at the same time to be trying to restrain. 'Sorry,' he gasped after some moments – 'sorry, I thought I could just ask you in the ordinary way, but when it came to it . . . I found I couldn't. Sorry.'

'Don't let it get you down, Adrian,' said Fotheringay. 'It was all trick photography, what you saw. Bloody amazing what they can do these days, you know. Must have cost somebody a fair packet, mind. But anyway, no call for you to fret like you're doing now.'

'No, but when he thought it was for real,' said Chatterton.

'Absolutely,' said Fotheringay. 'Oh no, I fully appreciate that.'

An awkward pause supervened, during which Adrian seemed to pull himself together and each of the remaining two waited for the other to proceed. In the end it was Fotheringay who nodded resignedly and spoke up.

'Er, Chatterton here and me, we got talking and we came to the conclusion we don't want to go on with this any longer. "This" being the kind of play-acting or pretend caper or make-believe we've been going in for up to now. Now we've got to know you a bit we reckon you've had a raw deal, and we're sorry, right? The thing was, we were both without a job, down on our luck, when this bloke comes along and throws cash around like he's got three arms and says there'll be more to come if we just look after somebody for a couple of days and go on according to this kind of script he's got for us, if you see what I mean. We say okay. But . . .'

Chatterton now broke in. Throughout what followed he stayed much closer to his police-sergeant persona than to the urbane self Adrian had first seen. 'The background is that Mr X had set everything up for a whole programme of unpleasant experiences aimed at punishing somebody he'd taken a real dislike to – lucky for you that you only got as far as the first of the series, there was a lot worse to follow. Then right at the last minute the job's off. The central character's suddenly not around any more.'

'Being as he's dead,' said Fotheringay.

'Anybody I know?' asked Adrian.

'Let's hope not, for your sake.'

'Keith Gordon,' said Chatterton. 'Also known as Big Thief. He had the misfortune to be under a couple of hundredweight of stonework when it fell off his office roof. Apparently it was a genuine accident.'

'I heard about it,' said Adrian.

'The word is he'd been warned it was unsafe but was too bloody mean to have it seen to,' said Fotheringay.

'Act of God,' said Chatterton contentedly. 'Who managed to get it right for once. Well now, Mr Hollies, imagine where that left our Mr X. He'd laid out oodles of funds and in the twinkling of an eye it was all going to be wasted. Or was it? In his shoes I know I'd have gritted my teeth and called it a day, but here was another one that didn't believe in money going down the drain. So how about a replacement for Big Thief? To cut what must have been a long story short, the best he managed to come up with was A. Hollies Esquire, a real swine who turned out to be a literary agent. Not that I'm trying to make you sound unimportant, Mr Hollies.'

'No, of course not.'

'Right. Anyway, what had you done to him?'

'I've never done anything much to anyone. What did he say I'd done?'

'I didn't deal with him direct, but there was something about gross professional misconduct.'

'In my part of the trade it's not worth cheating anybody. I suppose I could have told him a book he'd written wasn't worth publishing.'

'Could be, very well,' said Fotheringay. 'Something that don't matter, like a book. You remember I thought this bloke was crazy right from the start.'

'You said yourself it was out of proportion, didn't you, Mr Hollies? And have you ever physically abused a girl, as I was told last night? Of course you haven't.

135

Nobody could believe such a thing who saw you reacting to what you thought was the real thing. Oh dear.'

'There's not much time,' said Fotheringay. 'We've said we're sorry. We're going to wrap this up. But you understand, Adrian, we want to protect ourselves. We request – that's all we can do in the circumstances, request you to assist us. You're a clever sort of fellow and you know about things like stories and writing scripts and that. Now you just get down to it and write a story for, er, for Chatterton here and me to learn, right, showing how you got the better of us and got out of here. Clocked one of us on the head, kind of style, and made a fool of the other, get the idea? Best you can do in the next hour or two. We'll help you any way we can, I give you my solemn word.'

'What about Beaumont-Snaith and Llewelyn?'

'Yeah, well I reckon Llewelyn'll do what we tell him, don't you, Chatterton? As regards Beaumont-Snaith, he took a nasty bang on the head just now when we were discussing what to do, so could be he'll turn out to fit into the scheme quite smoothly. We'll just have to see how it goes, won't we?'

'Wouldn't it be simpler,' said Adrian, 'if we all just pretended to have gone through the whole programme?'

Fotheringay nodded slowly with eyebrows raised. 'Okay, but only if you fancy spending a couple of months pretending to be a nervous wreck after it, which is what you would have been. And us trusting you to do it, of course. No, I reckon we'd all be better off with Plan A.'

III

'And I presume Plan A went reasonably well,' said Derek Richards the following week.

'That's what I presume too,' said Adrian. 'We started off by cleverly buggering up the closed-circuit TV system, which naturally I'd assumed was there from the start. Then I luckily turned out to know a bit of karate, anyway enough of it to put paid to Beaumont-Snaith. Marvellous name, that. As for it going well, I've had no complaints, though I must say if I'd been one of them I wouldn't be feeling all that easy in my mind.'

'How about the doctor?'

'The ex-doctor was going to disappear somewhere abroad whatever happened, on account of a previous piece of his doctoring having gone seriously wrong, and duly did, in a flash. He was a real ex-doctor, by the way, quite a different figure from the others.'

'What tipped you off about them?'

'Well, the general way they spoke and carried themselves and the rest of it, as if they were on the green, in mummers' parlance. If you were brought up in a theatrical household as I was, it's unmistakable. You must have noticed, when you turn the TV on or switch channels at random, how quickly and certainly you can tell whether it's acted, however straightforwardly, or real life. I realised rather late on that those chaps talked like coppers in telly plays, not actual coppers, though that was right in a way, but I had plenty of time to take in that they were camped-up villains too. Then when Chatterton took two actorial phrases from me in quick succession without turning a hair I knew I was right, and confirmed it by firing a couple of lines from *Macbeth* at Llewelyn and getting a shock-horror reaction. He must have carried a spear some time in a rep production of the

Scottish play as they call it because they think it's bad luck even to call it by its right name, let alone quote from it offstage. They're all grossly superstitious.

'What else did I know about actors as a tribe? That they were fluent but slow on the uptake, conformist, emotional and sentimental, impressionable, above all impressed by acting, so wrapped up in the theatre that to see a part played with conviction, in other words hammed up a trifle, affected them more than the real thing ever could. So I set about acting my head off in the part of the decent, plucky little man who stands up to the big bullies even though he's scared to death and who can put up with his own sufferings but not somebody else's. And it went down a treat, didn't it?'

'Don't undersell yourself, dear boy. You showed some real pluck as well.'

'I found I could miss a lot of that film by rolling my eyes up. And it's easier when you're acting. I must go.'

'Where does Julie think you were?'

'With A.N. Other. She had a fling with S.O. Else so that's all right. We were having a difference at the time. I was only away for one night.'

Adrian left Derek Richards in his office and went upstairs to his own. He had not told Derek or anybody else about how, immediately on returning to his desk, he had telephoned that Pennistone whose pitiable book on the world of high finance he had so rightly dismissed out of hand, nor how he had given Pennistone notice of his return, just that and no more, nor how half a minute's complete silence at the other end of the line had been the only response.

Afterwards, Adrian had been as satisfied as he cared to be that he had identified the man Chatterton had stagily called Mr X and that there was nothing more to be expected from that quarter. He wished only, and that not

very ardently, that he could have known the where-
abouts of the house he had been taken to in a drugged
state and brought back from with his head, however
willingly, in a bag.

But there was one more thing. With the obstinate
punctuality of the unwelcome, Jack Brownlow arrived
no more than a couple of seconds after the agreed hour,
full of fraudulent apologies for taking up the firm's
valuable time. He settled himself down in a chair by the
window with a self-importance suggesting his conviction that, in the years that lay ahead, visitors to this office
would be told in hushed tones that that was the self-same
chair *Jack Brownlow* used to sit in. No doubt for a similar
reason he wore his usual archaic suit.

'Did you manage to glance at those rough xeroxes I
dropped in the other day?' he asked when he was ready
to.

'Yes I *did*.' Instead of going on to say that he had
thought he recognised them as the opening pages of
Brownlow's last novel, and had had to check to make
sure they were not, or not quite, Adrian went on to say, 'I
don't know how you do it.'

Luckily Brownlow made no offer to explain how. He
said, 'That's a relief. I just thought it was time I made a
clean break with the sort of thing the public expect from
me.'

Adrian made some reply. This time what he did not
say was that he had got an idea for a sort of thriller that
began with a kidnapping, something he would gladly
part with if Brownlow thought it was time he made a
clean break with the sort of thing the public expected
from him. Another lecture on how novelists should stick
to their own experience might be too much to bear.

Captain Nolan's Chance

A Play For Radio

Principal Characters (*denotes a fictitious person)

CAPTAIN LEWIS NOLAN *In his late twenties. An upper-crust Irishman brought up in Milan.*

LORD ROBERT CECIL *In his mid-twenties.*
[*later Lord Salisbury*]

CAPTAIN IVOR MORRIS *A few years older than Nolan. I see or hear him as a fairly posh Welshman. 'Ivor' is my invention. I cannot find Morris's true Christian name nor much about him, but a Capt. Morris certainly led the 17th Lancers at the charge, which he survived though grievously wounded, and was certainly a close friend of Nolan's and a fellow-enthusiast for cavalry.*

COUNT ROGACHEV* *In his thirties or forties.*

LORD LUCAN *Mid-fifties.*

LORD CARDIGAN *Late fifties. A 'plunger', an aristocrat who spoke with a distinctive jargon or accent, pronouncing R as W and interlarding sentences with loud and meaningless exclamations of 'Haw haw'.*

JOSEPH★   *In his forties or fifties. Speaks with an accent differentiating him from Russians, eg Polish or Ukrainian.*

LORD GEORGE PAGET   *In his mid-thirties. A gallant soldier, later a general.*

SIDNEY HERBERT   *'Secretary at War' in the 1852 cabinet of Lord Aberdeen.*

Sequence 1 – London

We are in Pall Mall in the year 1854. A cab draws up.

CABBY: Here we are, gents. Retrenchment Club. Oh, thank you, captain. You two gentlemen going to be off to fight them Rooshans?

NOLAN: One day, maybe.

CABBY: Well, give 'em a bang on the boko from me. Good night, sir.

The cab moves off. During the exchange NOLAN *and his companion have alighted. They cross the pavement, mount some steps and enter the lobby of the club. A* PORTER *approaches.*

PORTER: Good evening, gentlemen.

NOLAN: We're here to see Lord Robert Cecil. We are Captain Lewis Nolan and Captain Ivor Morris. His lordship is expecting us.

PORTER: If you'll be good enough to wait a moment, sir, I'll inform his lordship that you gentlemen have arrived.

NOLAN: Thank you kindly. (*A moment.*) Ivor, for God's sake: this fellow is younger than you or me. Sure he comes from a grand family and they say he's a coming man, but there's no side about him at all. He's always been interested in the Eastern Question, that's Turkey and Russia and the rest of it. And the lad's fond of horses, do you understand.

PORTER: (*Approaching*) Would you come this way please, gentlemen.

They walk through part of the club.

PORTER: Captain Nolan and Captain Morris, your lordship.

CECIL: Thank you, Hawkins. Thank you for coming, Nolan. So this is the estimable Captain Morris. All I know about you, sir, is that you're a childhood friend of Lew Nolan here, and that you share some of this mad Irishman's delusions.

MORRIS: I'm afraid there are one or two subjects, my lord, on which neither Lew nor I is quite sane.

CECIL: That's a relief. I pass my days with sane people and believe me it's hell. Now sit down and let's have a drink. The sherry here can just about be swallowed if you grit your teeth, or you might prefer a little brandy.

Fade down and fade up in the main dining-room of the club.
CECIL, NOLAN and MORRIS are at a table by themselves.

CECIL: What's being said about the appointment of Lord Lucan to lead the cavalry?

NOLAN: Well, unlike the other generals he has seen active service.

CECIL: Oh, I didn't realise that.

NOLAN: Twenty-six years ago. He did well enough then.

MORRIS: And then, on April Fool's Day, if you please, it's announced that Lord Cardigan is gazetted Brigadier-General in command of the Light Brigade. Now Lucan's a difficult fellow, but the word is he's a good tough officer. But Cardigan, he's . . . may I speak plain, sir?

CECIL: Please do.

MORRIS: Lord Cardigan is a lunatic, that's the kindest thing you can say of him. Arrogant, reckless, obstinate, brooking no opposition, a damn fool, and unfortunately as brave as a lion. And in the 17th Lancers I'm to be under his command. The thought of that frightens me.

144

NOLAN: Which doesn't often happen to Ivor Morris. And my lord Cardigan wants me as his personal assistant, his ADC.

CECIL: Are you going to take the job?

NOLAN: I'll see the fellow in hell first. You know, my lord, when I think that the British cavalry list is full of brilliant and experienced officers in the prime of their careers, not one of whom has been given a command in this expedition, because their service has been in India – well, I want to weep.

CECIL: Before you collapse altogether, Nolan, you'd better have a glass of port.

We have moved to the port-drinking room of the club. NOLAN *is well away.*

NOLAN: It's my belief that, properly led, cavalry, especially light cavalry, can do anything.

CECIL: Is it your belief that cavalry could break an infantry square?

NOLAN: Yes, even that – sir. There's not just the one key to it, but two. The first is the man; well, the British army knows about him and how to train him. The second is the horse, and the British army needs a lesson or two about how to train a horse.

MORRIS: You mentioned leadership, Lew.

NOLAN: That comes later.

CECIL: When we talked before, Captain Nolan, you mentioned kindness as the basis of your system.

NOLAN: That's it, my lord. A horse should never be punished or startled, but shown he can trust the man on his back. I'll see if I can find you a copy of my book, *Nolan's System for Training Cavalry Horses*, it's all in there.

MORRIS: I'm afraid Nolan is something of a fanatic on the subject, my lord.

145

NOLAN: Ah, to hell, you're as bad yourself, Ivor.

MORRIS: All right, I may be pretty bad, but I have to admit in all honesty that my lads in the 17th are second to none as cavalry soldiers, and even some of the Hussars are pretty fair.

NOLAN: Oh, they're not all hopeless.

CECIL: You think they'll give a fair account of themselves against the Russians?

MORRIS: I think so, my lord, yes.

NOLAN: If they get the chance.

CECIL: M'm. I hope you're right.

We are in the same place but time has passed. All three men are slightly foxed.

CECIL: I think one more glass, don't you? Well, no doubt we could go on about horses all night, but I didn't invite the two of you along here just for that. Let me put it briefly. Now perhaps Lew Nolan has told you, Captain Morris, I concern myself greatly with the activities of Russia in the Near East. I scent a grave threat to our interests there and further afield. This affair now in the Black Sea, it may prove to be no more than a skirmish, a preparation for something larger. There's a devilish crafty fellow in St Petersburg called Count Rogachev whom I don't care for the sound of one little bit. Very powerful in an underhand way and a deadly enemy of England and jealous of our possessions overseas. I see in him a grave danger to our country.

MORRIS: Lew and I promise to throw this Count Rogachev into the Black Sea as soon as we set eyes on him, my lord, but what can we do meanwhile?

CECIL: I'm sorry, I think I was a little carried away. What the two of you can do for me meanwhile, my dear Morris, is to compile a report for my eyes only on the fighting qualities of our troops – morale, state of training, whatever may signify. They haven't fought a serious war for forty years – how would they resist a powerful and determined foe? You've told me something already; I need to know more. Will you do it?

NOLAN: We'll do all we can, sir.

CECIL: As it comes to you, nothing fancy. The telegraph would be quickest, but you'd have to resort to code.

NOLAN: We'll find a way, my lord, never fear.

Sequence 2 – St Petersburg

We are in a reception room in a palace. Men and women are chattering and laughing, eating snacks and drinking. JOSEPH, *a dignified butler, is supervising the serving of drinks.*

JOSEPH: A glass of champagne, my lady? Your excellency?

EXCELLENCY: Thank you, Joseph. Always on hand when you're wanted, eh?

JOSEPH: (*In undertone to* SERGEI, *waiter*) Two champagnes, Sergei, quick. And a napkin.

SERGEI: (*Nervous*) Yes, Mr Joseph.

EXCELLENCY: Splendid stuff. Yes, my dear, I always say it's a blessing the French can't fight half as well as they make champagne.

LADY: They fought well enough under Bonaparte.

EXCELLENCY: Until our Russian lads broke their spirit. Before you were born, Tania. I was just a young subaltern then. Yes, and Wellington finished Bonaparte off at Waterloo. I doubt if any British army could manage such a thing today.

LADY: Have you visited the Crimea yourself, uncle?

EXCELLENCY: Not as yet. I hope to go in a week or so . . .

COUNT 1: Well, as for our armies in the Crimea, they have only to wait for the British and the French to die of cold and fever and thorough incompetence, especially at the top. Their Lord Raglan and the others are drunk from morning to night.

COUNT 2: As I see it, Prince Menschikov need only hold firm and use his guns whenever he can. Our Russian artillery will settle things, as always.

COUNT 3: Allies? The flower of England, France, Turkey and Sardinia, if you please. A pitiful polyglot rabble, sir.

ROGACHEV: (*Calling imperiously*) Joseph, over here.

JOSEPH: (*Calling*) At once, my lord count. (*To* SERGEI) Come, Sergei – when Count Rogachev calls, you move fast.

ROGACHEV: Yes, colonel, I think this news makes the prospects for our little scheme look quite encouragingly. (*To* JOSEPH) Some vodka for the colonel. No, just soda water for me.

JOSEPH: Here we are, sir. (*To* SERGEI) Some vodka for the colonel . . . Oh, bless my soul.

ROGACHEV: Joseph, if you've got a moment . . .

JOSEPH: (*Gamely*) Of course, your honour.

ROGACHEV: . . . just find my secretary, would you, and tell him to start assembling the select company straight away in the small parlour. And Joseph.

JOSEPH: Yes, my lord.

ROGACHEV: Of course we shall need refreshing there too, you know.

JOSEPH: Of course, your honour, I understand. (*To* SERGEI) Get those glasses changed at once, they're filthy.

SERGEI: Yes, Mr Joseph.

Fade down and up to small parlour. Half a dozen men are talking in low tones. ROGACHEV *comes in and all fall silent.*

ROGACHEV: Most honoured, your royal highness.

PRINCE: My dear Rogachev, I wouldn't have missed it for anything.

ROGACHEV: That's kind of you, sir. Well . . .

All sit.

ROGACHEV: Thank you all for leaving the party to come along here. I'll keep you away for as short a time as I possibly can. In fact I have only two points to bring before you for the moment. The first is that I'm now in possession of what I think is conclusive evidence of the low state of training and the very poor morale of the British forces fighting – if that is the word – in the Crimean peninsula. That's more important than—

GENERAL: Count Rogachev, may I put in a word here?

ROGACHEV: Please, let's hear your views, general.

GENERAL: Thank you. Well, fighting is certainly the word for what the English infantry were doing on the 20th of last month at the battle of the River Alma.

VOICES: Oh, that. Yes, we've heard a lot about that. Oh, the Alma.

GENERAL: Yes, the Alma. Those men showed not merely courage but blind courage in the way they went on advancing over the river and up those slopes in the face of withering fire from our guns, roundshot, grape and canister. They fell in masses but they kept advancing. Does that indicate very poor morale? Count Rogachev?

ROGACHEV: No more, general? Thank you. Accounts of that engagement seem to vary. Major?

MAJOR: My information is that the 'heroism' of the British has been somewhat exaggerated and mis-interpreted. We should not forget—

ROGACHEV: The British so-called heroism is something of a myth called into being by way of excuse for the incompetence and timidity of our own commanders.

149

GENERAL: Nonsense, they're both fine soldiers. I've served with 'em.

ROGACHEV: It's touching, isn't it, the way the army always stands together, no matter what. If I may just finish this point, the state of an army's infantry is a far less telling indicator than that of its cavalry, who are likely to be a little less brutish by nature. Of course I speak myself as a cavalry soldier . . .

VOICES: Quite right. Of course. Hear hear. About time too.

ROGACHEV: Thank you. And – the British cavalry is in such a state, despite its fine uniforms, that their generals dare not use it, it seems. Major.

MAJOR: Yes, my lord. At the battle of the Alma, which has made such a profound impression on the general here, the famous British cavalry stood by and did nothing. The previous day at the valley of the Bulganek, their Lord Raglan ordered their cavalry to retire before they had even drawn their sabres. What humiliation!

A handbell rings.

ROGACHEV: I beg your pardon, major. Please continue.

MAJOR: The rest is detail, my lord. The theme that emerges is that their cavalry are frightened of our guns.

Voices express assent. Double doors open and JOSEPH *and* SERGEI *come in with drinks.*

ROGACHEV: Ah, Joseph, quick about it, now. Champagne for His Highness, vodka, and for me I think a small glass of still white wine. Well, gentlemen, this comes at a timely moment. Consider the victory our Cossacks will win over the British lancers and hussars and dragoons when they meet on the great plains below the Himalayas! A toast – your royal highness, my lords, gentlemen, I give you – the imperial conquest of India!

VOICES: India! We'll show 'em! To victory! Long live the Czar!

ROGACHEV: Joseph, my trusty friend, you shall join our toast! Pour yourself a glass of wine and raise it on high!

JOSEPH: Thank you, sir, but I beg your lordship to excuse me. My wretched stomach . . .

Pause.

ROGACHEV: Oh, very well. But you should see a doctor about those insides of yours, do you hear me?

JOSEPH: Oh yes, your honour.

ROGACHEV: See to it. (*Raises voice*) Is it your wish that I put our plan before the High Command at their next meeting?

VOICES: Yes! As soon as may be! Don't let's delay any longer!

GENERAL: Have you a date for this Indian escapade of yours?

ROGACHEV: I soon will, general.

We are in a smallish office with an open window overlooking the Neva. Hooter noises, etc.

PEMBERTON: (*Friendly*) But you didn't manage to get the date.

JOSEPH: Not yet, Mr Pemberton, I'm afraid. It's not easy.

PEMBERTON: I imagine not.

JOSEPH: Especially not since Count Rogachev became watchful. I was a fool to get out of drinking that toast. I just couldn't . . .

PEMBERTON: What does he suspect, Joseph?

JOSEPH: Not the truth, or I wouldn't be here now. No,

he merely thinks I don't love him, which is true. I must be more careful to prevent him from seeing what I really feel about him.

PEMBERTON: How can you be sure nobody's watching you?

JOSEPH: Because I don't trip over a little man in a mask every time I turn a corner. It's strange how a people as deceitful as the Russians should be so bad at anything to do with spying. Don't worry, Mr Pemberton, I'll get you that date.

PEMBERTON: Well, it can't be for a few months yet, with winter coming on. In fact now I think of it . . .

He shuts the window.

PEMBERTON: That's better. What is it?

JOSEPH: I just hope you're right about those few months. I wouldn't trust Rogachev not to get troops over the Himalayas in dead of winter by balloon. Well, a little bit of judicious eavesdropping should settle the matter.

PEMBERTON *has opened and shut a drawer and now tosses a packet of banknotes on to the table between them.*

PEMBERTON: I'll look forward to it. You'd better count them.

JOSEPH: No need, Mr Pemberton.

PEMBERTON: Very well. You know, I think you'd do this work for nothing.

JOSEPH: Maybe. Maybe.

Sequence 3 – The Crimea

Near Balaclava, 17th October, 1854. In the distance a large force of Russian cavalry is manoeuvring back and forth. In the foreground a large force of British cavalry is advancing at a walk and trot. The troopers are chatting among themselves as they ride.

TROOPERS: Glory be, we're going to have a smack at 'em at last. We'll show those Russki swine who's master. About time too. Who do they think they are? Our turn now, eh?

SERGEANT: (*From near by*) No talking in the ranks. And watch your dressing there. Smartly now. Sit up straight and take a pride in it.

OFFICERS: (*From out in front*) Halt! Halt the 17th. Halt the Scots Greys. Halt the 11th.

The entire cavalry division halts.

SERGEANT: Right, settle yourselves, lads. Remember they're watching you. Prepare to charge. Now's the time to say your prayers. Listen to your orders, listen to the trumpeter, and do what you're told. Now, all quiet. Steady. And God bless us all.

Some moments pass in silence.

NOLAN: (*Muttering*) What the devil are you waiting for, Lord Lucan, you great ninny, you aristocratic booby, is it reinforcements from God's angels you're wanting? (*To colleague*) Will you just look at that ground now, boy, and tell me if you ever saw country better suited for a cavalry charge?

COLLEAGUE: You're right, Lew, it's ideal.

NOLAN: No narrow lanes, no woods, not as much as a damn hedge to jump, and as for the going, you couldn't wish for better at Newmarket. And we're all here. What's the matter with Lord Look-On? God, it's driving me mad.

COLLEAGUE: Keep your voice down.

More moments pass. Then the Russian cavalry in the distance start booing, jeering, laughing. Their trumpets can be heard.

NOLAN: The bastards are about to withdraw. I'll not stand it, so I won't.

He gallops off.

We are up with LORD LUCAN's *headquarters group, half a dozen officers with orderlies.*

STAFF CAPTAIN: They'll be forming column in a minute, sir. In order to retire.

COLONEL: Lord Lucan, I beg you, order the charge before it's too late.

LUCAN: I know your feelings, colonel, but you must know I cannot charge. I must follow what Lord Raglan has laid down. The Commander-in-Chief has stated most categorically that I must in no circumstances attack.

COLONEL: He's not here now, sir. It's a golden opportunity to deal a deadly blow.

LUCAN: Colonel, I have my orders.

NOLAN: (*Approaching*) Lord Lucan . . . Lord Lucan . . .

LUCAN: Who's this fellow? (*To* NOLAN) Who are you, sir?

NOLAN: Captain Nolan, at your service, my lord. Now if no one else will do so, I have to tell you to your face that by failing to attack the enemy when he's at our mercy you have neglected your duty, sir. Whatever your orders may have been, the responsibility of taking the war to the enemy is paramount and overriding.

LUCAN: How dare you, sir. Pray withdraw immediately.

NOLAN: You're supposed to be the general commanding the cavalry division, not a damn nursemaid. Back there are some of the finest soldiers in the world, and you're letting them just sit and chew their nails. You're a disgrace!

The last speech is broken into by protests, etc., from LUCAN, COLONEL *and* STAFF CAPTAIN. NOLAN's *last words are shouted as he is hustled away.*

LUCAN: I've a mind to have that insolent Irishman court-martialled.

COLONEL: I think it would do no good, my lord.

LUCAN: As I put it in my recent memorandum: It is not the duty of light cavalry needlessly, without authority, to engage the enemy.

COLONEL: Just so, my lord. Shall I have the Retire sounded?

LUCAN: Thank you, colonel, if you would.

COLONEL: (*To* TRUMPETER) Sound Retire.

TRUMPETER: Sir.

The trumpet-call rings out.
The waiting British cavalry hear the trumpet-call from the front. The men are furious.

TROOPERS: The Retire! I can't believe it. Damn that cowardly swine Lucan to hell! Some general. Lord Look-On is right. We'd have cut 'em to pieces. Aren't we ever going to get a smack at 'em?

SERGEANT: (*Shouting*) Silence in the ranks! (*To* CAPTAIN) You can't blame 'em, sir.

CAPTAIN: (*Shouting*) Squadron will move to the right in column. Squadron will retire, 3 Troop leading. Walk march. Smartly there! (*To himself*) Oh God.

Fade out cavalry moving at walk.

Sequence 4 – London

Official building in Whitehall or somewhere. CECIL *is walking along a corridor on the way to his office.* DANVERS *comes up.*

DANVERS: Good morning, my lord.

CECIL: Morning, Danvers. Has the mail from the Crimea arrived?

They walk along the corridor together.

DANVERS: On your desk, sir.

CECIL: The only thing in this whole mess and misery that seems to work is the mail service.

DANVERS: They say bad news travels fast, sir.

They enter CECIL's *office.*

CECIL: They're right there. (*Opens packet*) But for the electric telegraph we might still be living in a fool's paradise.

DANVERS: I hear, my lord, that in a few months we shall be able to get our news direct from Balaclava.

CECIL: If we still have anybody there to send it. (*Reading*) Oh dear.

DANVERS: I'll leave you, sir.

CECIL: Don't go far.

DANVERS *goes.*

CECIL: Oh, Lew, you are a positive wonder. More than just a clever fellow with a bribe. How do you do it? It's supernatural.

NOLAN: (*Voice fades up*) Greetings to my pious friend. Our bishop here is in very bad odour. Two days ago our loyal clergy were all keyed up to spread enlightenment among the heathen. It was a perfect opportunity. But alas, my lord bishop hummed and ha'd and did nothing. Our clergy were furiously disappointed. I myself remonstrated with my lord, who retorted with

156

dignity that he had specific orders from my lord the archbishop to refrain from any attempt to spread the holy word without specific orders. What can a true believer hope to do?

Our clergy are in a very bad state, the kind of sullen discontent that precedes real trouble. Unless they get the chance soon to do something effectively evangelical their spirit will be lost. This is very urgent. Please advise me. Your reverend friend and brother. PS The bishop from Wales is as usual. He awaits the coming of his yacht from England with his French cook on board.

CECIL: The bishop from Wales? Oh – Cardigan, of course!

Knock at door.

CECIL: Come.

DANVERS *enters.*

DANVERS: From Lord Clarendon's office, my lord, by special messenger.

CECIL: Thank you, Danvers.

                                        DANVERS *goes.*

CECIL: (*Opens envelope. Reads*) 'I thought you might like to see the enclosed. Please understand that it is a matter of the strictest confidence between us. G.V.' Thank you, George. Now—

PEMBERTON: (*Voice fades up*) Our man reports that Count Rogachev seems most interested and well informed as to the state of training and morale of our troops in the Crimea, with particular reference to our cavalry. This is no academic interest of his but an essential feature of his scheme to bring about a Russian invasion of India. A plan for this has been laid before the Imperial High Command, but our man is still unable to learn the proposed date of the move. What seems certain is that Rogachev sees as vital to his plan the supposed, or real, disinclination, or inability, of our troops to resist a determined and forceful adversary, especially . . .

CECIL: Especially where cavalry is concerned. Indeed. What else?

We are in a beau-monde London house during a party. Men and women are talking and moving about, e.g. up and down staircase.

HERBERT: Well, my dear Cecil, this is most pleasant, happening to run into you like this.

CECIL: It's good of you to say so, Herbert. For me, it's more than pleasant. You're the very man I was hoping to see.

HERBERT: You don't say. How delightful. Well, what can I do for you in the next couple of minutes?

CECIL: Very quickly – you remember this fellow Rogachev I was asking you about?

HERBERT: Rogachev? Oh yes, that Russian count fellow. What about him?

CECIL: That scheme of his for the invasion of you-know-where. What do the Cabinet make of it?

HERBERT: Make of it? They make nothing of it, Cecil. If they've heard of it at all, they've forgotten it.

CECIL: They think it of no account?

HERBERT: None whatever. Heaven knows what they do think of account. Keeping income tax down to sixpence in the pound, most likely. Well, must be off.

His voice is lost for a moment in the noise of the party. Then we hear it again.

HERBERT: (*Calling*) Oh Cecil!

CECIL: (*Approaching*) Yes, Herbert?

HERBERT: Just remembered – I was talking to a fellow in

the Horse Guards the other day, and your friend Rogachev came up in conversation. Apparently he tried to get into our Light Dragoons some years ago, and they turned him down. No leg for a boot or some such jargon. That's all.

CECIL: My dear Herbert, that is most interesting.

HERBERT: (*Fading*) Just thought I'd mention it.

CECIL *is in his office with* DANVERS.

CECIL: (*Dictating*) The Muscovite priest we spoke of . . . was once refused entry to one of our seminaries. Full stop. Hence perhaps his contempt for our clergy. Stop. Your remarks on their low spirits are noted. Stop. Recommend you do your utmost to encourage some demonstration of their superiority to the ungodly, comma, whatever your bishop or archbishop may say. Full stop. No, comma: or not say. Full stop. Would you read the last phrase back, Danvers?

DANVERS: Whatever your bishop or archbishop may say, or not say.

CECIL: Or not say. Whatever Lord Lucan or Lord Raglan may order you to do, or fail to order you to do. That is a little strong perhaps.

DANVERS: Shall I strike it out, my lord?

Pause.

CECIL: No. No, keep it. Address to Captain Lewis Nolan – HQ HM Forces – Crimean Expeditionary Force. Priority. And that means priority with you too, Danvers, so down to the telegraph office you go like a bullet.

DANVERS: Immediately, my lord.

He leaves.

CECIL: No leg for a boot!

He collapses in laughter.

Sequence 5 – The Crimea

The British forces outside Sebastopol. Before dawn on the 25th October. A bitterly cold night, wind howling, sentries stamping their feet, etc. NOLAN's *tent.* MORRIS *approaches it.*

NOLAN: That you, Ivor?
MORRIS: It's me right enough.

He enters the tent.

MORRIS: What a night!
NOLAN: At least we're out of the wind in here.
MORRIS: Did you hear we lost an officer last night? Major Willet. Dead of cold or exposure or whatever you call it.
NOLAN: I can believe it. Do you know, I wish I was in Balaclava town this minute. They've got fires down there. Girls too for all I know. And liquor.
MORRIS: *I* wish I was in Sebastopol, in the bloody fortress with the Russkis. Snug as a bug in a rug I'd be. With the occasional trifling inconvenience of a British shell possibly disturbing my slumbers.
NOLAN: Without the faintest chance of a British soldier coming to stir me out of 'em. When will they learn? It doesn't matter how long you bombard a place, you might as well be whistling at it unless you send a storming party in, horrible men with swords and bayonets and pop-guns to kill whoever's stirring. I wonder if the point ever strikes that perfumed idiot Lord Cardigan.

The British siege-guns are bombarding the Russian fortress of Sebastopol. LORD CARDIGAN *and a couple of* OFFICERS *ride up.*

CARDIGAN: Ah, I see. Those fellows down there are our

men, and they are firing at the Russians. Is that correct?

OFFICER: That's correct, my lord.

CARDIGAN: Yes. Well, why don't we drive them away?

OFFICER: We seem not to have the forces sufficient to undertake such a difficult operation, my lord.

CARDIGAN: I have never in my life seen a siege conducted on such principles. Or lack of them. Without an assault this cannonade is useless. Huge sums of money have been blown away in ammunition; time, which is of the most vital importance, has been squandered, and nothing whatever has been gained. What is to be done next?

OFFICE: We await orders from Lord Raglan, sir.

CARDIGAN: No doubt you do, my boy. Well, it's back on board the *Dryad* for me. Some miles away, it's true, but I might as well be back in Whitehall for all the good I can do here. And at least on my yacht I can be dry and warm.

Back in NOLAN's *tent.*

NOLAN: (*Fade up*) . . . and not counting the Sebastopol garrison, there must be twenty thousand Russian troops out there, infantry and cavalry and heaven knows how many guns.

MORRIS: Under General Liprandi, who it seems is an aggressive sort of customer.

NOLAN: I rather fancy the sound of him. It's worth crossing swords with a bastard like that, if we ever get within ten miles of him.

MORRIS: The Lord will provide.

NOLAN: He'd better. Otherwise we'll have to provide something ourselves.

MORRIS: You know, Lew, I've been thinking about your telegraph message from Robert Cecil. The last sentence, where he as good as told you to do anything you could to get our fellows a chance to hit the Russkis with everything they've got. Easy for him to talk like that in London, isn't it? I mean—

NOLAN: Oh, the lad's heart's in the right place, but he's never seen action.

MORRIS: Action, what action?

NOLAN: Sure, he's no notion what inaction's like either, British army-style, courtesy of Lord Look-On. Oh, it's hopeless, Ivor.

MORRIS: The only thing he can think of to do is get us all out of bed an hour before dawn to 'stand at our horses'. There's the aggressive spirit for you.

NOLAN: Right, let's go and stand at the poor nags. They must be as miserable as we are.

LUCAN *and his staff walk their horses through the gloom.*

STAFF OFFICER: All present and correct, my lord.

LUCAN: Thank you. Who's that?

PAGET: (*Calling as he approaches*) George Paget here, Lord Lucan.

LUCAN: Good morning, Lord George. Lord Cardigan not appeared yet?

PAGET: I expect he's still on his way from his yacht, sir. I'm deputising for him. Getting quite used to it.

LUCAN: Let's move on to the artillery emplacement. They may have news there.

They ride on.

PAGET: (*Surprised*) Hullo!

LUCAN: What is it?

PAGET: There are two flags flying from the staff. What does that mean?

STAFF OFFICER: Why, that must be the signal that the enemy is approaching.

PAGET: Are you quite sure?

A great cannonade of British [light] guns starts up. We hear sounds of battle but no close engagement.

LUCAN: If the Russians storm the heights there's nothing between them and Balaclava but our cavalry.

PAGET: What are your orders for the Light Brigade, Lord Lucan?

LUCAN: Lord Raglan has done nothing, not even sent word. It must be our first duty to defend the approach to the town of Balaclava.

PAGET: Orders for the Light Brigade, sir!

LUCAN: Lord George, you will take the Light Brigade into reserve.

PAGET: My lord, please give us something to *do*, something active.

LUCAN: Kindly carry out my order at once. I will go forward with the Heavy Brigade and the Horse Artillery to make threatening demonstrations and using my guns as long as my ammunition lasts. Forward, the Heavy Brigade!

Bombardment. Two great explosions. Sounds of Turkish infantry in retreat.

STAFF OFFICER: Lord Lucan, most of our squadrons have come within musket range.

LUCAN: So I see. I must withdraw the whole cavalry division to the slopes of the Causeway over yonder. Proceed by alternate regiments. Send an order to Lord George Paget.

Cavalry on the move.

CARDIGAN: Morning, Lord George. Beautiful day.

PAGET: It is now, my lord.

CARDIGAN: H'm. How goes it?

PAGET: Not well, sir. In fact damn badly. The Russians are out in overwhelming strength, all our gun emplacements have fallen, the Turkish troops have run for it, we've lost command of the heights, and it looks as though we're going to lose Balaclava too. And the cavalry division has been moved out of the way.

CARDIGAN: That wretched Lucan again.

PAGET: Not this time, my lord, in fairness. Specific orders from Lord Raglan. We were in an excellent position before. Now there's only a few hundred Highland infantry under Sir Colin Campbell and a few dozen Turks to face the Russians.

CARDIGAN: I've no confidence in any of 'em.

Russian cavalry on the move.

LUCAN: On the order of Lord Raglan, eight squadrons of dragoons under General Scarlett are to be detached from the Heavy Brigade towards Balaclava to support the infantry.

CAMPBELL *addresses his troops.*

CAMPBELL: Men, remember there is no retreat from here. You must die where you stand. But for the moment you don't stand at all. Everybody down flat and don't get up till I give the word. And when you do get up, both ranks be ready to fire. We'll give those Russkis the shock of their lives. Make sure every shot tells.

Russian cavalry charging.

CAMPBELL: On your feet, men! Front rank, aim! Fire!

Volley of musketry. Confusion among Russian cavalry.

CAMPBELL: Rear rank, aim! Fire!

More of the same.

CAMPBELL: Get back in line, there! Damn all that eagerness! Let 'em come to you! Front rank, aim! Fire!

More of the same, followed by Scottish cheers.

CAMPBELL: Had enough, you Russian dogs? Ay, get yourselves out of harm's way while you can! I don't blame you!

British cavalry on the move.

SCARLETT: Halt!

MAJOR: Looks as if we're not needed here after all, General Scarlett.

SCARLETT: What do you mean, major? What about that lot up there?

MAJOR: But that's the main body of the Russian cavalry, sir. Thousands of 'em.

SCARLETT: Well then, they won't be expecting an attack from a few hundred.

MAJOR: But they're uphill from us, and the ground between is badly broken.

SCARLETT: Two more reasons why they won't be expecting us. And look!

MAJOR: Surely they're not halting there.

SCARLETT: Preparing to outflank us. We won't give 'em time. Now's our moment, while they're not moving. Come on! (*He draws his sword.*) Trumpeter, sound the charge!

Trumpet sounds. SCARLETT's *force charge the Russians and a great fight ensues.*
The Light Brigade are halted not far away.

PAGET: Smash into 'em, lads! Well done, old Scarlett!

CARDIGAN: These damned Heavies will have the laugh of us this day, Paget.

PAGET: Not if we move at once, my lord.

CARDIGAN: Lord Lucan's orders are that we are on no account to leave this position.

PAGET: Can't we attack without orders, sir?

CARDIGAN: Who are you to ask such a question?

From among the great fight comes the sound of English, Scottish and Irish cheers as the Russian force breaks and flees.

TROOPERS: They're running for their bloody lives! We can cut 'em to pieces as they are now. Surely they'll let us forward? What are we waiting for?

MORRIS: (*Rides up to* CARDIGAN.) My lord, are you not going to charge the flying enemy?

CARDIGAN: Certainly not, Captain Morris, we have clear orders to remain here.

MORRIS: But, my lord, it is our positive duty to follow up this advantage.

CARDIGAN: No, we must remain here.

MORRIS: I implore you, do, my lord, allow me to charge them with the 17th. See, my lord, they are in disorder!

CARDIGAN: No, no, sir, we must not stir from here.

MORRIS: (*Turning away*) Gentlemen, you are witnesses of my request.

PAGET: We're all with you, Morris. But it's no good.

MORRIS: My God, my God, what a chance we are losing!

LUCAN *and his staff.*

NOLAN: (*Riding up*) Lord Lucan, sir, message from the Commander-in-Chief, sir.

LUCAN: Kindly read it aloud so that all may hear.

NOLAN: Sir. (*Reads*) Lord Raglan wishes the cavalry to advance rapidly to the front. Follow the enemy and try to prevent the enemy carrying away the guns. Troop Horse Artillery may accompany. French cavalry is on your left. Immediate. Signed by the second-in-command.

LUCAN: I see. Or rather I fail to see. I can see nothing. From here, neither enemy nor guns are in sight. I know the enemy are in possession of guns of ours captured at the emplacements, and there are guns, Russian guns, at the end of the North Valley with the remnants of their cavalry. Which guns are meant? And is there to be no infantry support? Cavalry to charge artillery? Absurd.

NOLAN: Lord Raglan's last words to me were that the cavalry are to attack immediately.

LUCAN: Attack, sir? Attack what? What guns, sir?

NOLAN: There, my lord, is your enemy, there are your guns.

LUCAN: The Russian guns. At the end of the valley. Very well.

NOLAN: Will that be all, Lord Lucan?

LUCAN: Thank you, Nolan.

NOLAN *rides over to* MORRIS.

NOLAN: Good day, Captain Morris. Are you now in command of the 17th?

MORRIS: Good day, Captain Nolan. Yes, my superiors are all off sick.

NOLAN: We are to charge the Russian guns. Have I your permission to ride next to you?

MORRIS: By all means . . . Lew – you mean those Russian guns down the valley?

NOLAN: It's our chance come at last, Ivor, our chance to show the world.

MORRIS: Oh. Very well. We must do what we can.

LUCAN *rides up to* CARDIGAN.

LUCAN: Lord Cardigan, in pursuance of this order from

the Commander-in-Chief, you will advance down the North Valley with the Light Brigade. I will follow in support with the Heavy Brigade.

CARDIGAN: Certainly, sir; but allow me to point out to you that the Russians have a battery of guns in the valley on our front, and batteries and riflemen on both sides.

LUCAN: I know it, but Lord Raglan will have it. We have no choice but to obey.

CARDIGAN: I understand, sir.

LUCAN: Advance very steadily and keep your men well in hand.

CARDIGAN *rides over to his staff.*

SERGEANT: (*Calling to* TROOPERS) Right, pipes out there now. Don't disgrace your regiment by smoking in the presence of the enemy.

PAGET: I hope that doesn't apply to me, sergeant. I'll wager there isn't another cigar like this in all Balaclava.

SERGEANT: I think it's up to you, sir.

PAGET: I don't want to set a bad example.

CARDIGAN: (*Rides up*) Lord George, we are ordered to make an attack to the front. You will take command of the second line, and I expect your best support – mind, your best support.

PAGET: You shall have it, my lord.

CARDIGAN: In the first line, the 13th Light Dragoons, 11th Hussars, 17th Lancers. Second line, 4th Light Dragoons and the 8th Hussars.

STAFF OFFICER: Very good, my lord.

The regiments form up. CARDIGAN *draws his sword.*

CARDIGAN: (*Quietly*) The Light Brigade will advance. Walk march. Trot!

The troops set off, clearly audible owing to a sudden lull in firing. Then the distant guns crash out. As the first shots arrive, wounded men and horses cry out.

NOLAN: Oh, what have I done? Sweet heaven, forgive me!

He pulls ahead of MORRIS.

MORRIS: Get back in line, Lew! We've a long way to go and must be steady! (*Shouts*) Come back!

NOLAN *overhauls* CARDIGAN.

CARDIGAN: Here, captain, get back to your place in the line! Captain Nolan, get back, I say!
NOLAN: Now hear me, all you men!

The rest of his words are drowned in explosions. A final one is very near. NOLAN *is hit. His horse wheels and begins to gallop back through the oncoming Light Brigade.*

MORRIS: (*Horrified*) Oh Lew! Oh God, oh God!

From NOLAN '*There burst a strange and appalling cry, a shriek so unearthly as to freeze the blood of all who heard him. The terrified horse carried the body, still shrieking, through the 4th Light Dragoons, and then at last* NOLAN *fell from the saddle, dead.' The tumult of the battle fades to nothing.*

CARDIGAN: That fellow Nolan behaved like a damned insubordinate dog, Scarlett. And a coward, too. Imagine the fellow screaming like a woman when he was hit.
SCARLETT: Say no more, my lord; you have just ridden over Captain Nolan's dead body.

Sequence 6 – London

A convalescent home. CECIL *is visiting* MORRIS.

CECIL: You look remarkably well, Morris.

MORRIS: Yes, my lord, I probably do, for a man who's had his head cut open here and there.

They laugh ruefully.

CECIL: How long will they keep you in this place?

MORRIS: I think they want to see me walk before they decide.

CECIL: (*Tentatively*) If it's not too soon to ask you – what do you think happened at Balaclava?

MORRIS: Well, my lord, Lew Nolan was never an easy fellow to understand. He was behaving very oddly even for him when he rode up beside me just before the charge. But I've no doubt in my mind that about as soon as he read Lord Raglan's order he decided to misdirect Lord Lucan. A great chance for Lew to test his theory about cavalry.

CECIL: But he underestimated the Russian artillery.

MORRIS: And his own feelings. Poor Lew hadn't seen as much of the business of war as I had, and I reckon the sight of what those first shells did to our fellows and their horses was too much for him. It was a horrible reminder that cavalry are flesh and blood, not just part of a theory. I think when he was hit he was in the middle of telling us to turn back.

CECIL: (*Slowly*) Do you think he was influenced by my notion of bringing about something that would show our friends in St Petersburg the quality of British cavalry, their high morale and their bravery?

MORRIS: I couldn't say for certain, my lord, but I know he was powerfully impressed by it. Especially by your last message. He'd set his heart on proving you were right.

CECIL: (*Heavily*) I see.

MORRIS: My lord, have you heard whether the news of the charge has had any effect . . . back there?

CECIL: Not as yet.

Sequence 7 – St Petersburg

ROGACHEV *and his faction in conclave.*

ROGACHEV: Surely this 'charge of the Light Brigade' shows little but the blind stupidity of the British cavalryman.

GENERAL: It may or may not show that, Count Rogachev. What it certainly shows is miraculous discipline and magnificent courage.

ROGACHEV: So you witnessed it, general?

GENERAL: Your honour must know that I had not the opportunity. Nor the privilege. But a soldier need not be a witness of such a thing. For a soldier, to be told is enough.

ROGACHEV: We must beware of attaching too much importance to a single event. What is it, major?

MAJOR: I did witness that event, my lord count, from behind the battery which the Light Brigade were attacking. With all respect to the general, you have to see such a thing. Such a thing! (*Begins to break down.*) It was without parallel, it was unique, it was indescribable. The French general who saw it said it was magnificent, but it was not war. It was indeed magnificent, and it was war besides. (*Weeping*) Those noble fellows! If only we had ten such men in all Russia . . .

171

ROGACHEV: There, there, my poor major, what you need is a drink. (*Rings handbell*) Again, we must pay attention to the larger picture.

GENERAL: The larger picture is that, far from the British soldier being in a bad way, it is the Russian. Every man in our army, high and low, is dismayed and daunted and in a state of fear at the thought of an enemy who can do such things. We shall lose the war in the Crimea, we shall never defeat Turkey while she has such an ally, and India is safe from us while the British remain.

The double doors open. JOSEPH *enters with* SERGEI.

ROGACHEV: Ah, Joseph. Drinks for everybody, please. Champagne for his royal highness . . .

JOSEPH: At once, my lord. (*To* SERGEI) Champagne here . . . vodka here . . .

MAJOR: (*To* GENERAL) If you call for a vote now, sir, you will assuredly carry the day.

GENERAL: Will you support me?

MAJOR: Of course, and not only I.

GENERAL: Very well. (*Raises his voice*) I move that we petition the High Command to proceed no further with any plan to move against India. I call for a show of hands.

ROGACHEV: Immediately, general?

GENERAL: If it please your honour.

ROGACHEV: So be it. All present, please signify. For the general's motion, that the Indian plan be called off forthwith.

Hands are raised in silence.

ROGACHEV: Against, that we are still resolved to move against India.

Another pause.

ROGACHEV: In the circumstances I will not call for a toast.

PRINCE: Better luck next time, Rogachev.

ROGACHEV: I thank your royal highness for an impeccably British sentiment. (*Irritably*) That will be all, Joseph.

JOSEPH: Thank you, my lord count.

Sequence 8 – London

The Retrenchment Club. We move over to where CECIL *and* MORRIS *are sitting.*

CECIL: Well, Morris, you look well enough to take a glass of port.

MORRIS: Thank you, my lord. I think I could manage just the one.

CECIL: I suppose one or other of us has to say a great deal has happened since we last sat here.

MORRIS: Yes.

CECIL: Do you mind talking about it?

MORRIS: No. No, not all, my lord.

CECIL: Can you tell me how many were lost in the charge? The reports I've seen disagree.

MORRIS: I know for a fact that 673 officers and men began the charge. Afterwards, only 195 answered at the first muster. I was not one of them, and many unwounded men had lost their horses and only turned up later. Altogether 113 men were killed and 134 wounded. But for the French attack that followed, there would have been many more.

CECIL: A hundred and thirteen too many.

MORRIS: Oh, most certainly, my lord, but what would

you? And if it's any comfort, Lew Nolan would very
likely have done just as he did do if you had never met
him. He was a mad fellow.

Closing notes of the Last Post.

CECIL: Theirs not to reason why, theirs but to do and
die. But not in vain.

PS to Captain Nolan's Chance

Ever since I first heard of it as a boy, I have suspected that the charge of the Light Brigade at Balaclava was the result not of a blunder but of somebody's intention. My recent look at the matter in some detail has confirmed me in this view. For instance, Cecil Woodham-Smith's excellent, very full study, *The Reason Why* (1953), leaves one with at any rate a strong suspicion that Captain Lewis Nolan deliberately and vitally misled the commander of the Cavalry Division, Lord Lucan, about the objective of the charge.

Nolan had a unique chance to do so. He was the ADC of General Airey, Lord Raglan's second-in-command and the officer who wrote down and signed the fatal message that Nolan delivered. Up on the heights overlooking the battlefield, Raglan and Airey and their staff, who included Nolan, could see both (1) the captured British guns Raglan actually intended the Cavalry Division to recapture; and (2) the Russian artillery battery at the far end of the North Valley. From his lower position, Lucan could see neither (1), an easily attained objective, nor (2), to be attacked only at great risk. He was thus vulnerable to Nolan's deception (and had negligently failed to acquaint himself with the Russian groupings).

The reason why Nolan misled Lucan, if he did, would clearly have been something above and beyond his amply documented zeal for action. He was also a fanatical believer in the unrealised powers of cavalry, especially light cavalry. This too is well documented; after a dazzling early career as a cavalryman he wrote not one but two books on the subject, and much of what I put into his mouth in the first sequence of my play is a close paraphrase of some views he expressed. But for good measure, and to contribute something of my own, I invented a small conspiracy that included Nolan and plotted to convince a sinister Russian cabal of the formidable fighting qualities of the British soldier, especially the cavalry soldier.

Two points might be added here. I hope my conspiracy and its doings are fun, but in the end I incline to the view I attribute to Morris in his last speech, that Nolan as portrayed 'would very likely have done just as he did do' if there had been no conspiracy. And as for whether the historical Nolan really misled Lucan on purpose, we shall never know. Still, I rather think he did. True, he had a lot of luck with the incompetence that surrounded him, but it was the sort of luck that comes the way of murderous maniacs.

With exceptions like Nolan's discourse, most of my London and St Petersburg scenes (sequences 1, 2, 4, 6–8) are fiction. The Crimean sequences, 3 and 5, are largely factual, here and there closely so. For instance, Nolan's face-to-face diatribe against Lucan, Cardigan's remarks about siege warfare, Paget's questions about the significance of the two flags (and the cannonade that interrupts them), Campbell's words to his men, Morris's exchange with Cardigan, the text of the order to Lucan (verbatim), Nolan's placing himself beside Morris, Lucan's talk with Cardigan just before the charge, the incident of Paget's cigar and Cardigan's orders immediately following, the momentary lull in firing, the circumstances of Nolan's death and what Cardigan and Scarlett say about it afterwards are all matters of record. That record comes chiefly of course from what survivors of the battle wrote about it subsequently, and if one sometimes feels that they remembered with advantages, the capacity of human beings to say memorable or melodramatic things at great moments should not be forgotten.

Morris's version of the numbers killed and wounded in the charge is taken from p. 272 of *The Age of Reform* (1938) by E.L. Woodward.

1941/A

I – The Pacific Operation

. . . The Imperial Fleet that sailed from the Kuril Islands in the last days of November was the most powerful naval force ever assembled. It consisted in the first place of eleven battleships. The largest of them, *Yamato*, in which Admiral Isoruku Yamamoto flew his flag, was at 68,200 tons displacement one of the two largest battleships ever built, the other being her sister ship *Musashi*, then uncompleted. Each of their nine 18.1-inch guns (the biggest ever carried afloat) fired shells weighing 3,220 pounds. Top speed was a remarkable 27 knots to a range of 7,200 miles.

With the exception of the sister ships *Nagato* and *Mutu*, each bearing eight 16-inch guns, the other battleships in the Grand Fleet carried 14-inch primary armament, altogether providing a broadside of eighty pieces. Speeds of 22.5–28 knots could be attained. All the above ships could launch up to three aircraft via catapult.

The accompanying carrier component was likewise uniquely strong at the time, consisting as it did of no fewer than nine vessels, from the impressive sister ships *Soryu* and *Hiryu* with their capacity of seventy-one aircraft each and their top speed of 34.5 knots, to the smaller *Taigo* with her twenty-seven aircraft and 21 knots. In aggregate these ships carried the prodigious total of 380 aircraft.

Six heavy cruisers, fourteen light cruisers, sixty-six

destroyers and nearly one hundred other craft, including a sufficiency of tankers for refuelling purposes, accompanied the capital ships.

Divided into four forces under vice-admirals, this unparalleled armada set its course due east. It passed hundreds of miles to the north of the main Pacific base of the US Navy at Pearl Harbor, the objective of an earlier strike plan now superseded. The change of plan had been largely the personal doing of Yamamoto, who had never wavered in his conviction that Japan could only hope to defeat America in a short war, the shorter the better.

Thanks to miracles of organisation and the most rigid security, the Grand Fleet assembled intact and on schedule off the Californian coast, far enough off to be below its horizon. The four forces maintained for the voyage across the Pacific Ocean had become two, separated by some hundreds of miles, in fact the distance between San Francisco and Los Angeles.

At first light on 11th December, the Japanese fleet commenced bombardment of these two prosperous and populous cities with every gun that could be brought to bear, while every aeroplane capable of flight took off on bombing and strafing missions into their harbours and business and residential quarters. Complete surprise was attained. Of the initial salvoes, one heavy shell struck almost the precise centre of what was at that time the longest single-span suspension bridge in the world, opened only four years earlier, the Golden Gate Bridge at the entrance to San Francisco harbour. The bridge sustained great damage and there was some loss of life.

After a prearranged interval, the two forces ceased fire, turned into line abeam and steamed inshore, a change of location designed partly to permit greater accuracy and to conserve aircraft fuel, but also, at least as important, to leave the helpless citizens in no doubt of who and what it was that brought them destruction and death. The ships of the battle-fleet went to their new stations and recommenced bombardment, whether of the cities themselves or of shipping and harbour and other installations. The aerial attacks had continued without pause.

Shortly before 10.00 hours a tender or other small boat was observed approaching the waterborne forces bearing a rough-and-ready white flag. This impudent excursion, which could have claimed nothing conceivable in the way of legal standing or significance, was swiftly and properly dealt with. On orders of the Admiral himself, the destroyer *Shimakaze* closed with the intruder at top speed and rammed her amidships, cutting her clean in two. The remnants rapidly sank, those persons who had survived the impact being helped on their way by small-arms fire and grenades from *Shimkaze*'s deck.

By then or soon afterwards, large parts of both cities and their outskirts were ablaze. Visibility on this clear, sunny winter's morning had at first been excellent; now heavy clouds of smoke drifted across the target and ascended hundreds of feet into the air. Massive explosions occurred at intervals. One especially severe and prolonged disturbance in the San Francisco area has been taken to indicate a seismic shock induced by the bombardment in an area notoriously subject to earthquakes, but material evidence is lacking.

Despite increasing difficulties of ranging and targeting, the Japanese warships and warplanes prolonged their assault on the two coastal cities until breaking off the action shortly before noon. Already large parts of the afflicted areas had been destroyed, and hundreds of thousands of their people lay buried in the rubble or lay dead or dying in what had been their streets. Sentimentalists have suggested that the attack was needlessly prolonged and excessive damage and slaughter inflicted, perhaps forgetting the first objective of the Californian operation, viz. the delivery of the maximum possible shock, not only locally but throughout the United States. It could be asserted with some confidence, in the light of subsequent events, that those Americans who lost their lives in and around Los Angeles and San Francisco did so, albeit unknowingly, in the service of their country.

When the cease-fire came and all aircraft were safely returned, the fleet drew off. The whole of it with one exception began the long voyage home across the Pacific under the command of Vice-Admiral S. Toyoda. The exception, the giant battleship *Yamato*, whose ammunition had been conserved, started off on her way to a fresh target some 3,500 miles to the south-east, a target of such importance that Admiral Yamamoto had insisted on attending to it personally.

The naval forces assaulting the Californian cities had met with negligible resistance. A number of obsolete US warplanes made feeble, uncoordinated attempts to close with the vastly superior Japanese aerial armament, but in almost all cases these were shot out of the sky at ranges too great for them to return effective fire. Even considered solely by the standards of warlike profit and loss, the Pacific operation was the most successful in history.

II – *The Atlantic Operation*

Twenty-one hours in real time after the Japanese had launched their first attack, at first light on 12th December, the German battleship *Tirpitz*, having eluded the vigilance of the Royal Navy in slipping out of European cover and crossing the Atlantic, commenced bombardment of the city of New York.

At 41,700 tons and with eight 16-inch guns as primary armament, *Tirpitz* was clearly a ship on a rather smaller scale than the mighty *Yamato*, and hers was a solitary adventure; nevertheless the damage and loss of life she inflicted were considerable and bore closely upon events.

Tirpitz concentrated her fire on the island borough of Manhattan, though she caused some damage to the US Navy Yard on the farther side of the East River. Her shells destroyed or severely damaged several of the city's loftier buildings, including the 102-storey Empire State Building. Two considerable fires were started. At a later stage, making up in boldness for what she lacked in firepower, *Tirpitz* actually sailed some distance up the Hudson, bombarding the shore at point-blank range with every gun available. A salvo from her secondary armament of 5.9-inch guns reduced the famous Statue of Liberty to fragments.

Amid growing but still largely ineffectual signs of resistance, *Tirpitz* discontinued the action just before 0900 hours and retired. Out in the North Atlantic once again she turned southward, her mission in that ocean not yet accomplished. While in transit she successively launched from her catapult the four aircraft she carried, each of them an Arado 196A-3 twin-float seaplane carrying two 110-pound bombs. The two-man crews had been carefully selected and intensively trained for what was perhaps the most important part of the entire Western operational sector.

It had been decided with some reluctance that a regular naval attack on Washington, DC, though infinitely tempting, must be ruled out as too hazardous. Approach via the Potomac River or the Chesapeake Bay was finally rejected as too difficult and remote, with a risk that the encroaching force might be trapped and destroyed before it could withdraw. Such an outcome was unacceptable in view of the necessity that the enemy be denied any countervailing success, however small in proportion, on this day of his humiliation.

Accordingly, the four seaplanes delivered a short-range, low-level and deadly accurate attack on the White House on the late afternoon of a day that had filled it with Service and civilian chiefs of every description. No one who witnessed it would ever forget the unheralded approach at nearly one hundred yards per second of a warplane flaunting the insignia of a distant but hostile Power and firing a machine gun as it came. The story goes that one such round, penetrating a conference room by its shattered window, struck the wheelchair in which President Franklin D. Roosevelt sat and, ricochetting, hit and killed an air-force general standing behind him. Whether literally true or not, the supposed incident has great metaphorical force.

After completing a number of strafing runs at their target, and having dropped on it their collective bomb-load, amounting to something not far short of half a ton of explosive, the seaplanes rendezvoused with the *Tirpitz*. Two airmen were lost. Those killed in and around the White House ran into scores, but the moral effect of such a daring stroke was incalculable.

Now, by an assiduously reconnoitred route, *Tirpitz* continued her long journey to the south. Round the tip of Florida she steamed, through the Yucatan Channel between Cuba and Mexico, then down the Caribbean to her third and final objective.

III – *The Combined Operation*

During the night of 16th/17th December, *Yamato* and *Tirpitz* took up their stations off the two ends of the

Panama Canal, each vessel out of range of the shore defences. At a previously agreed time close to first light, both commenced bombardment of the sections of canal nearest them. After two hours the *Tirpitz*, whose primary ammunition had started to run low, discontinued fire, and a little later *Yamato* followed suit.

There were altogether six double locks in the canal system, each of great mass and strength. All lock walls rested on rock foundations and were over 80 feet in height. In the case of the outermost locks, the walls contained over two million cubic yards of concrete. Nevertheless the concentrated broadsides of the two great battleships caused multiple breaches in both. What with severe consequential flooding and damage to permanent installations, it was estimated from reports reaching the Washington office of the canal that, even under normal conditions, repair and reopening could be expected in months rather than weeks.

Before the preliminary investigations were complete, *Yamato* and *Tirpitz* had reached home and safety, having accomplished their part in the shaping of history.

IV – *The Sequel*

The Empire of Japan had declared war on the United States of America in a proclamation date-timed 11.30 pm on 11th December, but unfortunately delayed for some hours before it reached the US Government. At two o'clock that afternoon Joachim von Ribbentrop, as Foreign Minister, had read out to the American chargé d'affaires in Berlin the text of Germany's declaration of war.

The combatant Powers continued in a state of war seven full days. At 11.00 am on 18th December, President

Roosevelt delivered an address to both Houses of Congress and, by simultaneous radio broadcast, to the nation at large. The text ran, in part:

It is with a heavy heart, my fellow Americans, that I stand before you this day. You will all share my feelings of shock, sorrow and indignation at the appalling carnage that resulted from the Japanese surprise attack on the cities of Los Angeles and San Francisco. The German raids on the East Coast cities of New York and Washington, DC, though smaller in scale, were no less dreadful and demoralising. In the nation's capital I myself came under enemy fire, for a single instant only, but long enough to kindle in me a special sympathy with those men, women and children who really suffered.

America was still reeling from these heavy blows when the news arrived of the virtual destruction of the Panama Canal. That canal . . . is in a very real sense America's lifeline. Denied it, my Service heads advise me that the possibility of one day defeating in war two such powerful and such implacable adversaries as Imperial Japan and the German Third Reich is not non-existent but is hopelessly small, far too small for the substantial risk of total defeat to be run. Therefore, as your Commander-in-Chief, I hereby order all American forces to lay down their arms totally, finally and forthwith, pending the signing of a peace treaty. My fellow Americans, the war is over!

Now, I call upon you all to join with me, at this late hour, in returning henceforth to our traditional path of neutrality amid foreign conflict. Let us forgo any thought of revenge and pursue the proud role of beacon of liberty and democracy, by whose light other nations may in the end return to the paths of peace and goodwill.

Necessary adjustments in the status of certain of our overseas territories, and in some of our domestic arrangements, are in the process of being settled and agreed. As soon as the details shall be finalised . . .

The adjustments referred to by the President turned out to comprise the cession to Japan of all America's Pacific territories, including the Hawaiian Group with the Pearl Harbor base, Guam and Wake Island, and to Germany of Puerto Rico, while the Panama Canal Zone passed under the tripartite authority of the United States, Japan and Germany. The domestic arrangements concerned were naval installations in the continental United States. The US Navy was to be progressively reduced to fishery-protection and coastguard vessels.

When these details were after some days released to the American public, some revulsion of feeling occurred, and there were riots and disturbances from ocean to ocean, though not as violent or prolonged as those that followed the original bombardments.

Besides, it was too late.

From *A History of the Second Great War, 1939/A–1943/A*
by Michael Bridgeman
Josef Goebbels Professor of Modern History
in the University of Oxford